Let it be duly noted, I could not do any of
what I do without the staunch support
of my patient, understanding, and very
talented husband, Mike McPhail.

Other titles by
Danielle Ackley-McPhail

THE ETERNAL CYCLE SERIES
Yesterday's Dreams
Tomorrow's Memories
Today's Promise

THE ETERNAL WANDERINGS SERIES
Eternal Wanderings

THE BAD-ASS FAERIE TALE SERIES
The Halfling's Court
The Redcap's Queen
The High King's Fool
(forthcoming)

Baba Ali and the Clockwork Djinn
(with Day Al-Mohamed)

The Literary Handyman
Build-A-Book Workshop
More Tips From the Handyman

The Ginger KICK! Cookbook

SHORT FICTION
A Legacy of Stars
Transcendence
Consigned to the Sea
Flash in the Can
The Kindly One
The Die Is Cast
(with Mike McPhail)

# The Fox's Fire
## And Other Fantastic Tales

# Danielle Ackley-McPhail

Pennsville, NJ

PUBLISHED BY
Paper Phoenix Press
A division of eSpec Books
PO Box 242
Pennsville, NJ 08070
www.especbooks.com



ISBN: 978-1-949691-73-3
ISBN (ebook): 978-1-949691-72-6



"The Fox's Fire" originally published in *The Planetary Series: Venus*, edited by A.M. Friedman, published by Subversive Press.

"The Promise of Death" originally published in *Were-*, edited by Patricia Bray and Joshua Palmatier, published by Zombies Need Brains Press.

"The Devil in the Details" originally published in *Heroes of the Realm*, edited by Danielle Ackley-McPhail, published by Realm Makers Media.

"Forever and a Day" originally published in *Fantastic Futures 13*, edited by John L. French, published by Padwolf Publishing.

"Crossroads and Curses" previously published in *Trails of Indescretion Special Volume #3: Between Darkness and Light*, Fortress Publishing.

"Mis En Place" originally published in *Pangaea III*, edited by Michael Jan Friedman, published by Crazy8 Press, 2020. The Pangaea universe and all places, characters, and events therein are the sole property of Museworthy Inc, this story reprinted with permission.

"Mama Bear" originally published in *Bad Ass Moms*, edited by Mary Fan, published by Crazy8 Press.

Interior Design: Danielle McPhail
Cover Art: Fantastic Fox in Dark, gouache paint © Dr. Akkulak, www.shutterstock.com
Cover Design: Mike McPhail
Copyediting: Greg Schauer

# Dedication

To each and every one of my backers.
Project after project, you show your support
and your faith in me. That is humbling.

I cannot thank you enough.

# CONTENTS

# The Fox's Fire

*"A fox is neither human nor beast,
but an inhabitant of the space between."*
From "In Mystical Taiwan: Fox Spirits"

RYOKO MOVED LIKE THE MORNING MIST THROUGH THE CHERRY blossoms, silent, unnoticed, but with the swiftness of the summer storm winds. Her mouth gaped sufficient to reveal the tips of her needle-like teeth, deceptively delicate, as was the rest of her. A growl rumbled in her throat as she scented a strange beast on the morning breeze.

She paused at the garden gate of her honored household, crouched and ready. Then the chickens' panicked cries disturbed the dawn. Fresh blood scented the air. Ryoko ran forward, teeth fully bared. Her tail bristled and her legs went stiff as she came face to face with what appeared to be a *yako*—a wicked fox. Only Ryoko's eyes narrowed. Something *other...* foreign and magical taunted from beneath that fur. Slaughtered chickens lay scattered at his feet and blood dripped from his muzzle, which gave the impression of being spread in a grin. In her head she heard laughter, as dark as the *yako*'s black pelt. He stepped away from the carnage and sat, curled his tail around his feet, and began to bathe, making it clear he'd savaged the fowl for mere sport.

Outraged, Ryoko lunged forward, her jaws snapping to close upon his throat but nipping only air. Cunning stared back at her from tawny eyes. Again, the impression of laughter as the black fox leapt straight in the air and spun away, his tail whipping tauntingly in her face. She gave chase, following the wrongdoer far across the earth and even the ocean to a land she had not seen before. The *yako* evaded her, but she remained at his heels nipping and yipping. He pranced just out of reach, more as if he led than fled. But to what purpose? Ryoko's eyes narrowed and she nearly stopped her pursuit, not trusting this intruder from a foreign land, only the black fox spun and nipped her nose sharply before giving another laughing cry and dashing away. All intention of giving up the chase left Ryoko's thoughts and she pursued him to his native land.

Suddenly, as his feet hit the soil of that other land, the wicked fox changed before her eyes, black fur flowing away until he wore a tawny hide, his legs lengthening as his body took on a rangy look, standing first on four legs then on two, a mingling of canine and man. Her mind named him Coyote, a trickster god of whom she had heard before, even in her far-off land. He loomed over her, menace in his gaze and stance, but only for a fleeting moment. Instinct had her drop into a crouch, her ears pinned. The moment she cowered, the menace was gone, and mischief again lit his gaze. The Trickster took the form of the beast once more, pranced and laughed in a barking cry before vanishing before her eyes.

Ryoko was left puzzled as to why he'd so clearly lured her here.

She would have left this place herself, only a group of native men crept from the forest around her, bare but for leather leggings girding their hips. They had copper skin, not golden, their muscles flexing as they moved through the forest bearing weapons, clearly on the hunt, as she was. One stood out, capturing her attention first by his wild, golden eyes, then by his strength and pride, which were pleasing to her. He paused to look her way, almost as if he sensed her.

"Tokalo..." *Fox*—one of the other hunters murmured low in their native tongue, "what is it?"

The leader shook his head and waved the other man silent before proceeding forward.

Ryoko cloaked herself in mist, crouching as they passed, alert to their surroundings, but not her presence. Attracted by his intelligence and perception as much as by the burnished glimmer of his copper skin, she forgot her retribution and followed the native man, drawn to him more with each passing moment. Before she could pursue, she felt herself drawn into the pocket realm, her fox self reverting to her kitsune form.

"You cannot have him."

Ryoko flinched at the sudden, soft-spoken words as the Eldest One appeared beside her. The youngest whined, deep and low in her throat, desperate not to be heard. If they could have in her current form, her ears would have flattened down.

This was no fickle whim. He was meant for her. She knew it. Even his name, *Tokalo*, decreed it. In his own Dakota language, he was branded "fox." Surely, he was marked as hers from the moment of his naming.

The urge to beg the eldest was strong, but such would not serve Ryoko well.

"Come, child, it is time to go home."

"May I not even play a while?" the kitsune asked softly, her tip-tilted eyes lowered in respect, choosing a seemingly trivial tack as the surest to gain her desire. After all, if she could but be with him, she had no doubt the eldest would then see their love was destined. Ryoko schooled her face into a faint and charming pout; one that had for centuries softened the old one's heart. In silence, she peered out from the veil of her black-tipped, fox-red hair.

Chourou's gaze hooded in response. At her back there was a flicker; faint, as if of the afterglow of a thousand tails of flame fanned by a fractious wind. It was gone in an instant. Ryoko nearly wrinkled her nose at the fanciful thought. No kitsune known had more than nine tails to their honor. Only legends of legends spoke of more. And yet it took effort for Ryoko to remain still as the eldest pursed her lips. Every instinct told her to cower, to flee.

But that was not the way to gain her heart's desire. Ryoko remained steadfast.

After a long moment, Chourou let out a soft sigh. Satisfaction came to Ryoko's heart as the lines of the eldest's face smoothed and her chin tucked in the slightest of nods.

"For one night you may go to him, child, but keep nothing of him for yourself..." The eldest pinned her with a gaze. "This you *will* promise me."

Ryoko's dainty pout deepened a moment into a less-practiced expression, but she nodded, eyes still lowered, if only to hide her annoyance. She just managed to keep her fine brow from scowling.

"Yes, Chourou, I promise." It was inconvenient, but she was confident the eldest would recant the charge later.

A slight frown came over the old one's face and doubt tinged her gaze, as she waved Ryoko on her way.

Lips spread in a gamin grin, the young woman yipped her joy and with a twist and a leap she passed a broken leaf over her head and transformed into a fiery vixen, five tails fluttering behind her as she dashed away. This new wrinkle called for some forethought, lest in grabbing for a fleeting moment she lost a greater opportunity. In one bounding stride she disappeared into her private haven, a pocket realm she had created within the cap of an acorn: a secluded glade much like one in the territory of Tokalo's tribe.

The eldest shook her head as she watched her youngest of daughters caper away. *That one burns bright,* she thought, *fierce and fast and none too long. She will not see six tails behind her if she continues thus, let alone nine.* How could the young one grow beyond the five she had when she took no heed of wisdom? And yet there had been no point in denying the child. She was willful. Refusal would have triggered all manner of mischief, and who knew how much harm. Enough of that loomed with Coyote breaching lands he had no call to. What he wanted with her youngest Chourou did not know, but she would watch closely. The first step had been taken to foil the Western spirit. By consenting, the eldest gained Ryoko's promise—and promises must be kept. And, perhaps, some wisdom might be learned.

*There is no more to be done,* Chourou told herself. *May it be enough...* With a tense quiver she made her own transformation—without the aid of reeds or broken leaf—moving off in the opposite direction, her gait stiff-legged and anxious, her multitude of pale gold tails twitching at her back.

One night was nothing to squander. Twelve hours hardly seemed enough. Ryoko's tails lashed and she paced fretfully. She left no paw prints on the enchanted ground, but her spirit felt heavy with the weight of her promise, chafing at the unexpected burden. Frustration was bitter on her tongue and she had to forcibly restrain herself from unmaking the glade. Many were the hours that she'd spent here, peering out into his world, watching, learning, coming to understand Tokalo and his People. This place was special to her, but...

She was tired of watching.

There had to be a means to keep her promise *and* have her heart's desire. Ryoko refused to believe otherwise. An unconscious whine sounded from her throat. It was time to leave her pocket realm and begin the chase. As she unfolded time and place, her dainty paws came to rest on the soil of the mortal world until she pranced among the ferns that were the template for her glade.

She would not go to him... not yet. Her jaw lowered in a vulpine smile, and her *hoshi no tama*—the white globe housing her soul—glowed from between her dainty teeth, gleaming bright against the muted colors of the forest. One night only, she had promised. One night to *be* with him. No limit was placed on her time to court him from a distance. To taunt and tease until *he* sought *her.* That would surely grant her time enough to find a way.

Creeping from the stand of trees that grew around the creek, she raised her nose to the wind, then lowered it to the ground, searching for the scent of her chosen mate. When she captured it, she trotted eagerly across the plains. Pondering the challenge, the kitsune remained hidden as she followed his trail, employing illusion when she could not stay among the tall grasses. In her fox form it was not difficult to shadow him as he wandered.

There was something about his scent that disturbed her, though. A hint of musk that teased her senses with a faint trace that came and went. In its absence, her fox self wanted to twine around him in a sensual brush of fur and limbs. But when that certain aroma tickled her nose, it set her on edge, made her want to run back to the woods and hide deep in a burrow, curling her limbs until her snout tucked deep beneath her tail and no glint of eye could betray her. The scent put her in mind of a predator, akin, but not of a kind, with herself. For a brief moment she thought of the false *yako.* The next, of Coyote, something *other* and much more dangerous.

Puzzled, she slunk low and for a while forgot about courtship and seduction.

It was some time before the quiet of the plains soothed her. Eventually she came out of her crouch, her delicate tongue lolling in the heat as her bright eyes tracked Tokalo, admiring his pleasing form, the strength of him. His well-oiled muscles and the lean power that tempted her each time he moved. His skin was burnished bronze, and his long braids were black and glossy in the sun, like a bear's pelt, yet looking as soft as a black fox's fur. In form, he seemed perfection, but there was something about him... something that called for caution.

It wasn't until she spied her chosen crossing paths with some young women of his tribe that Ryoko realized she must act soon. At first, she ignored the maidens. They were an annoyance with their coy tittering and ducking of heads as they passed by on their way toward the creek. But then Ryoko noticed several making doe eyes in Tokalo's direction. She bared her teeth when she caught sight of that and turned her attention full upon them, ready to harry them away. Only she could not miss the fact that Tokalo stopped, his eyes tracking the women as they moved off. Was that interest Ryoko saw in his gaze?

She snapped her jaws upon the air in frustration. *She* needed to draw his interest. *She* needed to intrigue him. Once she managed that she could ensure that to him no other women existed. It would be as if the two of them shared their own private world.

*Their own private world...*

And in that instant, she knew what she would do. How did one make a night last forever? Ryoko's ears flattened to her skull, embarrassed at how she'd nearly overwrought herself when the answer was so simple.

Chourou did not say *whose* time Ryoko was to count by. One of Tokalo's nights spent in a pocket realm of Ryoko's construction would honor her vow, while allowing them years instead of hours. Surely that would give her cunning time to find the key to securing their forever.

Sly eyes narrowed, Ryoko studied the maidens as they departed, memorizing their style of dress, their hair, their mannerisms. One in particular continued to glance back several times, her gaze hungry and bold. Ryoko fixed that one's face in her memory, growling low in her throat willing the sound to carry to the threshold of the woman's hearing until that one jerked back around with a frightened squeak and hurried after the others disappearing among the trees.

With a course set, Ryoko relaxed, then became a little playful. She remained still and silent as Tokalo prayed with the dawn, but as he went about his tasks the rest of the day she no longer flitted quietly behind. She frisked among the undergrowth, flirted from the bushes or the tall grasses. Allowed him to catch brief sight of her... as kitsune... as woman. Never much and never long, but enough to start a courting dance, to make him aware. Fleetingly, she caught his eye and let the passion in her gaze speak as boldly as that other maiden's. On the wind she whispered to him; told him of her love in soft words he could only almost hear, like the murmur of the breeze among the cherry blossoms of her homeland. From time to time, she caught the ghost of a smile edging his lips. It was somewhat bemused.

They continued this way for some time, weeks, then months. Ryoko became Tokalo's other shadow. In the summer, the Siouan tribes gathered together on the plains. With so many others not of his tribe nearby, Ryoko was less guarded with her actions, not as concerned she would be singled out as a stranger. Sometimes she let Tokalo see her full, at a distance, but mostly just in glimpses; never beneath the sun, or near a fire, lest her fox's shadow betray her nature. Even so, he must have sensed something. At first his eyes were wary, then curious. When interest blossomed, Ryoko took to bathing beneath the moonlight knowing he watched from the trees. One night he called to her in his native tongue:

"Woman, I would be with you."

Ryoko the woman chuckled deep in her throat, coy, not cruel, then dropped quietly beneath the cool water and swam to the far side of the creek, passing reeds above her head. On four dainty feet, Ryoko the fox climbed to the shore among the bushes where he could not hope to see her.

The formal courtship had begun.

For several weeks they repeated this dance, Ryoko more reckless... bolder; Tokalo more determined... hungrier. Ryoko found it increasingly difficult not to speak and signal the next stage he expected in their courtship. One night she caught that disturbing musk just as she sought to slip away into the forest. She stilled, crouched low, jerking as a coyote's yip sounded all too near. Her movements rustled the ferns feathering her calves. Ryoko swallowed a gasp, her eyes darting glances through the twilight. Was that a common beast, or her nemesis? Though no sound betrayed him, Tokalo's scent grew stronger, edged in that nervous-making musk. Panicked, Ryoko dove into her pocket realm to evade her suitor.

The nearness of her capture left her panting in her private glade. Delicate ears tipped her head and a pink ribbon of tongue lolled from the corner of her fine, pointed muzzle, for all that her eyes and face remained in a human seeming. Fear eroded her control of transformation while longing made her careless. Perhaps now was the time to bring the chase to a close... but she was not ready for an end to their courtship. She was not ready for her one night only. What if her cunning proved false? What if fate counted the hours as hours, no matter the realm? Ryoko whined, fretful as her spirit refused to settle on one course.

And then something whispered across her thoughts. Feather light, like the tip of a fox's tail just brushing her skin. *Are you not kitsune? Are you not a spirit of the flame? Fierce and strong and beyond the touch of Man, if you wish it so?* Something about the encouragements were eager, almost anxious in their effort to persuade, and with them came phantom memories of the musky scent that plagued her.

And yet... the musings fanned Ryoko's pride. A frown settled on her face as by force of will she passed a broken leaf over her head and brought herself back to the aspect of a woman. Enough of games. Cloaked in the seeming of a Sioux maiden, Ryoko stepped out openly onto the plains, joining the gathered tribes around the fire many nights after the one where she'd fled.

She looked across the circle and met Tokalo's heated gaze. For once she allowed the ghost of a smile to grace her lips before lowering her chin to watch him demurely through her lashes. He snared her gaze a long moment, then spun away, disappearing into the darkness surrounding the tipis. Shuddering, Ryoko turned her attention back to the circle. As she tried to enjoy the chants and the dances, there rose a faint commotion beyond the circle of the People. Murmurs and gasps traveled like a lit fuse.

The moment Tokalo walked into the light thrown by the fire, now dressed grander than any of those gathered, with his manner solemn... ceremonial... Ryoko could not miss the challenge etching his strong expression. Low and deep, a drumbeat started, at first barely heard, then growing louder and louder. It grabbed her heart and drew it along at a frantic pace. Her suitor jumped into the steps of a rousing dance... graceful, powerful, heated... Ryoko could not look away. She watched him as he leapt and spun, stomped the earth mercilessly, drew his arms up as if he would take to the sky, then slashed them down again as if he would cleave the air. In the background the People chanted, but only Tokalo danced, until, with the sudden, rapid pounding of the drum, he soared across the flame to land proud before her. His skin glistened and his eyes burned.

"Woman, I would be with you," he murmured for her ears alone. "I would have you as my wife."

Joy. Sorrow. A thread of inexplicable fear. In spirit, Ryoko's ears flattened and her belly hugged the ground as Chourou's words echoed in her mind. *"You cannot have him."*

Yet Ryoko's heart said, *he is already mine.*

Then, this close to him for the first time, she noticed what she'd missed all times before. Scenting the air, she flared her nostrils. The kitsune woman whined and shivered, then took a half step back.

*Turn away,* she told herself, *do not say a word. You do not acknowledge his suit until you speak.* She knew this much from her watching.

Tokalo frowned.

Shocked murmurs sounded faintly around them, growing louder. Ryoko barely noticed as she realized what she'd smelt before, in the woods and many times after... then, as now, there were traces of Coyote on the air, his true scent mingled with the one he'd worn as the *yako* when he had first led her to this place. It colored Tokalo's fragrance and lent his form the glow that first drew her gaze. Though she could not see his shadow she would not be surprised if there were two. Her chosen had something of the spirit realm about him.

And then it came to her. Her anxiety faded to nothing. Perhaps this was her proof. What better mate than she for one spirit-touched? Surely all the signs decreed it so. All but her promise...

Her heart betrayed her. She looked up into his taut, proud face. Even as her honor screamed a silent "No!" her acceptance slipped past her lips. "Yes," she murmured back, love's warmth surging in her breast.

*You cannot have him...* the specter of Chourou admonished again.

*He is already mine...* Ryoko's soul persisted in arguing back.

Torn by this battle within, and sensing a threat she did not understand, Ryoko turned and fled too fast for Tokalo or the confused People to hinder her. The moment she was beyond the fire's light she whined and twisted and disappeared into her pocket realm with all five tails tucked behind her.

No more would she allow herself to shadow her love. No more would she flirt with him from the rushes. Ryoko watched him from her haven during the day, her heart aching more each time he called out to her as he searched the plain for the trail not even the greatest hunter could follow. Of a night she hid herself among his fire's flame, staring out at the hurt hardening Tokalo's features. Long he searched for her and long she hid. Shame filled her heart to see him suffer for her actions. A nameless dread stiffened her limbs and at her back her five tails thrashed without ceasing. Two vows she had spoken. Two promises as yet unkept. Her spirit weighed heavy with the burden.

Honor demanded she respect her word, whatever may come in the end.

Tension drained from her body as she bowed in acceptance. Carefully she prepared herself as a bride of Tokalo's tribe, adorned in a white doeskin dress finely beaded and heavily fringed. She bound up her feet in moccasins she had stitched herself and plaited her hair, glossy with bear grease, though it gleamed sufficiently on its own. Then, at the moment the sun next set, Ryoko stepped out of the darkness into the fire's light.

Slowly she began to dance, then much faster as the drumbeat took up its cadence. She carefully mirrored the steps her beloved first offered up to her, even to the leap across the fire, save she ended on her knees before him, head bowed, silently begging his forgiveness for fleeing.

Again, he murmured for her ears: "Woman, I would be with you, I would have you as my wife."

And Tokalo lifted her up and they were wed.

As she looked into her husband's eyes all Ryoko's thoughts of cunning fell away. She would take her one night with this man and not devalue what passed between them by cheating for more. And so, the kitsune embraced her Fox and loved him as no man had been loved before or since. In the flicker of the mortal fire, they came together in a joining of bodies and souls. She worshiped his form and offered herself up as tribute to his love. As the flames died down to embers, Ryoko wept unseen even as Tokalo rained tender kisses upon her and joined their bodies. Her eyes closed as the sun's rays began to lighten the tipi's hide. Her body stiffened at Tokalo's gasp. His name fell from his lips, though Ryoko had no doubt he spoke not of himself. Reluctantly she met his gaze. In his golden eyes she saw the reflection of her own face, then that of her fox features.

Realization dawned. Tokalo was a man of faith. His devout nature was proof against her magic seeming. In the light of day, he saw her as she was.

The whining keen that pierced the air was equal parts woman and fox.

She could not keep what belonged to another.

Ryoko held Tokalo's gaze... shuddered at the moment of hurt in his expression.

"I'm sorry, my love," she murmured, "but I must now go away." And with that she assumed her kitsune form, the glowing white orb of her *hoshi no tama* nearly choking her as she tucked her head and folded herself into her pocket realm.

She could not say if truth or longing placed the echo of Tokalo's cry in her ear or brushed his fingertips across her fur in an effort to draw her back.

Nothing broke through Ryoko's sorrow for the longest of time. Nothing, that is, until a familiar musk invaded her private space and enveloped her, jerking her from the depths of her sorrow. Ryoko growled deep in her throat.

"You were warned, child, that you could not have him."

Ryoko looked up into Coyote's lolling grin; nearly ignoring the warning in his golden eyes, so like Tokalo's, and yet not. Her muscles bunched beneath her until he spoke again, his words knocking her from her feet.

"Or any part of him..."

And the Trickster of all tricksters reached out, a satisfied smirk upon his lips. "I will take what is mine, now."

Ryoko scurried back as truth revealed itself. Her breath seized in her throat as she sensed the faintest of embers kindled in her core. Tokalo had joined more than their bodies within her. His seed had taken root and now Coyote sought to claim their young as his own, as she suspected had been his plan all along.

Snarling she rose from four legs onto two, her face that of a woman but her garb that of a warrior of her land. At her back crackled not five, but *six* fox tails, each of them whirling balls of flame into the air. Her heart broke at wisdom's price for that spiritual elevation. Already she felt the swell of her belly beneath the plates of lacquered bamboo armor. Perhaps Coyote was right that she could not keep the kit with her, but in no way would she concede it as his.

"My vow," she said in low, firm tones, "was to keep nothing of him for myself."

Before triumph could blossom on the Trickster's face, she continued, her heart racing with a fear she dare not show.

"The little one I keep in trust for her father, until she is ready for his world."

And with Ryoko's words came a flash of golden light, as of a thousand kitsune tails fanning the air.

"Heard and witnessed," came Chourou's voice at Ryoko's back, firm with the strength of a thousand plus years. "Now away with you, Trickster, before I decide my robe needs a new fur trim..."

Snarling, Coyote fled, a canny gleam in his gaze that Ryoko did not like. Some thought would have to be given to her child's protection when she went to be with her father. For now, Ryoko sent a stream of fire balls after Coyote but found no satisfaction in his faint yip.

As the image of him faded, Ryoko's muscles trembled with the heartache flooding her chest. When Chourou's arms came around her, Ryoko shuddered and loosed the keen rising from her throat. "I am proud of you, my child," Chourou murmured against her hair.

Ryoko found little joy in her elder's praise, or even in the prized sixth tail curled tight over her back, hard-won with bitter wisdom. Without a word she sent away her armor and folded herself around her silk-clad belly. She would have her child only as long as it sheltered in her womb. Such sorrow was too strong to let anything of joy take root.

In the months as her child formed, Ryoko filled the silences with professions of her love, told her little one stories of her parents' courtship, imparted all the instruction and comfort she had to give when she had none of her own to hold onto. She worried for her daughter and bent her thoughts to safeguarding the little one even in her absence.

When the birthing came Ryoko cried out with more than a woman's pain as her child was born into the world. With the cord barely tied she cradled the babe in her arms, placed a mother's kiss upon her brow, and folded herself into the between place from which she'd watched over her husband these long months past.

Knowing his heartache and the anger that had only just begun to fade, Ryoko waited to act until Tokalo sat alone in his sweat lodge, deep in meditation. She watched as he ladled a dipper of water over the flames, sending steam billowing from the heated rocks.

With a thought, she sent the embers at the base of the hot stones flaring again until a blaze rose up in their place as if the fire had never been doused. From among the flames, she peered out, her narrow face and her fiery tresses untouched, wreathed gently by the fire. She smiled at Tokalo, eyes burning with fresh tears beneath a flutter of long lashes, and as his gaze widened in awe, she raised her slender form half out of the fire's caress.

"Woman," he croaked in a voice harsh with disuse. "Why did you leave me?"

"For but a night you were mine, but forever I will hold you in my heart."

"And why have you come back?" Reluctant hope flavored Tokalo's words.

Ryoko forced the words from her grief-thick throat. "I am forbidden to keep any part of you for myself," she told him as she drew back her arm and its full, sheltering sleeve, to reveal the bundle cradled in the other. "And so, I have brought Takara to you and would have your vow that you will keep our daughter safe and love her as I would."

Stunned, her husband stared in wonder at the giggling babe she placed in his arms, perfect and unharmed, playing with a familiar glowing white orb. She had her father's dark gold eyes and her mother's shock of fox-red hair.

"Look for me within the flame, my Tokalo, for I will ever be close by to watch over those I love." Ryoko's gaze flickered to the child as she attempted to suckle the orb. "My heart and soul remain with both of you always."

#  The Promise of Death



AN RÓGAIRE RESISTED THE URGE TO RUB WHERE A CRESCENT-shaped ivory sliver yet marked his forehead, hidden by a dark shock of once-silken hair now gone rough. Just enough horn remained to serve as a stark reminder of all he had lost. Magic... kin... his true form... even his name. Everything but his life—which felt all but worthless without the rest—and his new-found purpose. A muscle in his cheek twitched as he raised his head and flared his nostrils to sample the air.

He caught a whiff, a mere memory of his quarry's scent, faint and growing fainter.

Tension radiated up his jaw as his teeth clenched. With each passing day the threat grew that Den Jeger—brother to the man who had died severing An's horn—would figure out how to use it. Not an alicorn alive would be safe as long as Jeger held his trophy. Much like a dousing rod, the spire would lead the hunter to anyone nearby with even a trace of magic, alicorn or otherwise.

An would not let that happen. Just the thought drove him closer to the edge of madness as rage flared through him. He was more than a touch mad anyway, as most alicorns robbed of their horns—and thus their magic—tended to be, but for the most part he was able to stay on the reasonable side of sane. In part because of the sliver of horn left to him, in part because he must. Forcing back the pain at the center of his forehead, An turned his focus outward and hunted the hunter, not for vengeance, but to neutralize the threat.

Jeger had to be stopped.

The energy of Dublin grated on An like a constant jolt applied directly to his nerve endings. He liked the city and had visited often over the years, but this constant exposure wore on him. What he wouldn't give to leave the perpetual barrage of traffic sounds, human voices, and electronic noise for the gentle music of the wild, to run on four legs and not two. Just for half an hour. Instead, Jeger lead him a merry chase through the city. Over the last week they'd stalked one another back and forth across every neighborhood in Dublin.

For now, An had lost track of the hunter. Snarling, he cut down an old, cobblestoned alley heading toward Trinity College, trying with the meager magic still at his call to locate Jeger's trail... or the spire's to be more precise.

An had been both blessed and cursed when he'd been cleaved. Once most rogues transformed to their human form for the final time—the only defense a hornless alicorn had in humanity's world—their ability for magic was spent. Not so for An Rógaire. The sliver he had left allowed him enough ability to glamour his features and cast other minor workings—such as sensing the inherent magic in others... and his horn, which Jeger had taken as a trophy. All An wanted was to retrieve the blasted thing and have done with this half-existence. No... that wasn't precisely true. What An truly wanted was to pound Jeger beneath his hooves until his fetlocks were crimson with the man's blood, to hear the man's screams fade away into the squelch of pulping flesh...

An's footsteps became more forceful in response to the violent thought and his lips twisted in a cruel smile, until those walking toward him began to swing wide to go around.

As he realized it, he abruptly stopped, trembling as a cold, clammy sweat coated him. This was not him. This was not the behavior of an alicorn, whose nature was to heal, not harm. With each day that passed—and with him hardly realizing it—the madness took more control.

He needed to end this before it was too late. Before these impulses extended not just to Jeger, but to all mankind. Once the threat was gone, An could let go and find... release... from this shadow existence.

For that he had to find Jeger.

Recklessly, he overreached himself, grasping for magic beyond his current capability. His stomach churned with the effort and a piercing pain lanced through his head. Slumping against a worn brick wall, he heaved a sharp sigh and pressed the heel of his hand against his forehead where the scar throbbed.

"Soundin' mighty vexed there, sunshine."

An jerked upright, his hand tightening into a raised fist. Aggression briefly surged through him, until he forced it back. As he regained control, he recognized Charlie's voice and felt a phantom sensation down his back reminiscent of the tingling brush of another's magic. A sensation An had not felt since his cleaving. As his nerves settled, he nearly snorted as the misnomer registered. But then, his friend here tended toward snark. "Nearly missed you today, Charlie," An said in his gentlest tone as he forced his hand to relax. "Not finding trouble out there, are you?" As he spoke, he reached into the messenger bag slung across his shoulder and drew out what would have been his lunch. He managed an impression of a smile as he leaned out and handed it to the waif.

With a sullen look, Charlie jerked a hard head shake as she all but grabbed the sandwich. "Got more sense than that, An Rógaire."

He flinched. Though that alias predated his losing his spire, it was the only name he had claimed since. Being addressed by it left him feeling raw, as if he lost a little more of himself each time it was used.

Charlie didn't even notice, all her attention focused on the food. Deft hands extracted half the sandwich from the wrapper and squirreled the rest away, somehow managing to do so in a way that made it seem nothing was there at all. If not for her age and obvious state of existence, An would have suspected Charlie of being one of his kind, but no foal could have mastered the human transformation this young, and even if one had, they would have been sheltered and nurtured, not cast alone into the world to subsist among humankind at such a tender age.

Still... perhaps somewhere back in her human lineage she had alicorn kin. Despite living on the rough there was a sense of purity there, and signs of mage potential that might develop as she grew older. It was enough to make him wonder.

Of course, Charlie's entire nature was a puzzle to him. A long tenure on the streets had made her age and sex nearly indeterminate. Any tell-tale features were as hidden as the sandwich he'd given her. Most people assumed she was a young boy. An figured somewhere in her early teens and female, but that was just instinct. Her scent was muddied, not clearly one gender or the other. He'd known her for years through a mutual connection to the local Romani clan, but even he couldn't be completely certain, though he was better equipped than most at sensing biological cues.

Without intending to, he leaned a little closer and let his nostrils flare, still trying to make sense of Charlie's scent. She tensed and her jaw stilled. Though they'd known each other a while and counted each other friend, Charlie never lost the sense of self-preservation that kept her alive on the streets. She looked ready to drop the food in her hand and bolt.

An caught himself before she took off. He stepped back out of reach to lean against the opposite wall of the alleyway, sliding his hands into his pockets and crossing his ankles. It almost wasn't enough, but after a long, taut pause, Charlie lifted the sandwich and made half of it disappear in one bite, never once taking her eyes from him.

"What's the word?" he asked, knowing street kids—especially this one—were better informed than practically anyone else, just as a matter of survival.

That got him an eye-roll and half-shrug as Charlie carefully chewed, then swallowed before answering, showing she had more sense than most of those he sacrificed his meals to. An reached into his bag again and drew out a bottle of water, which Charlie was quick to take, but not snatch. She sipped enough to clear her throat before answering, then squirreled away the rest.

"The yobs are causin' trouble down by the docks, an' a new crop of Paki dossers are settin' shop 'round the market. I tell ya, they could teach them cinema actors a thing or two, they're that good at fakin'. Oh, an' someone's snatchin' schoolgirls, but it's real strange. Always good girls... lily white, if ya get me. They turn up somewhere a few days later loopy or somethin' but otherwise just fine. Three's gone missin', an' two's come back so far."

An bobbed his head and let her ramble between bites until her sandwich was gone. Normally this was the point where they'd part ways. An hesitated. What she said about the schoolgirls concerned him, but that didn't sound like Jeger's thing. Yet anxiety twitched down An's back in an instinctive warning he couldn't shake.

It wasn't like anyone would confuse Charlie with a schoolgirl. Hell, as far as he knew no one except him pegged her as female at all. If this was a random snatcher, An was pretty sure she was safe.

But what if this wasn't some random perv? What if gender wasn't the only common identifier between the victims? Jeger was out there somewhere roaming those streets Charlie called home. That made An nervous. He still couldn't say if his young friend had anything to worry about. Might be there was nothing more than the usual; unless his suspicions were correct and she was an aliman, a melding of their kind with threads of magic woven through her humanity. That could definitely put her more at risk from the hunter. The horn fragment Jeger possessed could lead him right to her thinking she was alicorn... and worse yet, if she had any developing mage sense, she might not realize a stranger drew near if she felt An's essence through the horn.

Again, violent urges surged through him. He closed his eyes as he felt them begin to roll and clenched his jaw as he swallowed down a bugling scream. Breathing slow and deep, he got himself under control before he spoke.

"There's a man out there you need to stay clear of..."

Charlie scoffed. "Just one, An?"

"I mean it, Charlie," he said, leaning forward to catch her gaze. "This guy's a hunter and might be you have enough in you of what he's hunting for." An quickly described Jeger, from his brush-cut blond hair to his flat brown gaze. He detailed the scar across the hunter's right wrist—for which An was unintentionally responsible—and even the horn shard—though An didn't call it that—which never left its custom-made sheath at Jeger's side. The way the man moved and how he operated. The words came out in a rush because An didn't know how long she'd let him talk before taking off. He could feel himself losing his calm with each word. Already her eyes were wary. "If you hear anything about him... or worse, cross paths with him, stay clear and get word to me through the Clan."

"Don't know what you're going on about." She started to back away and he knew she'd dash once she was clear of the alley.

"I just want you to be careful, Charlie. He's after me, but that doesn't mean you're safe if he notices you... If he notices what I have."

An spoke that last to the empty air.

Tension rippled through every muscle and drew his brow into a vicious scowl. An felt something looming on the air. As if there were somewhere he should be. Driven, he made his way across the Temple Bar. His hands fisted and his shoulders bunched as his gaze tracked all around him. Where was the bastard? It wasn't like Jeger to drop off the grid. To taunt and tease and try and lead An somewhere society wouldn't interfere, that was the hunter's usual course. But Jeger was nowhere to be found.

Jeger's absence left An agitated. But that wasn't all.

Over the past weeks three more girls had been reported missing. They had all turned back up, in the same condition. Innocent girls, unharmed and intact, but with no memory of what had gone before. He had a bad feeling Jeger, misguided by legends of unicorns and virgins, was responsible for the abductions after all.

That wasn't why An was worked up, though. What had him worried was that there were only six girls reported missing. And seven had been found.

The seventh was a street kid no one knew or cared had gone missing.

An couldn't help but think of Charlie, whom he feared was number eight. The otherness about her reminded him of his own kind. The only other instance a human came close to such a resemblance—without possessing magic—was those who were pure.

Like all the other girls gone missing.

Alicorn had no care for human abstinence; what they sought was their own kind. Unfortunately, one form of purity often mimicked the other, giving rise to the legends.

The thought that the hunter might have targeted his friend kindled rage in An's belly. He felt the urge to roll his eyes and toss his head, rearing up in a display of equine fury, though his body could no longer manage the posture and his rough, shoulder-length locks hardly constituted a lashing mane. He fought the impulse down, but it kicked his ass. Even in the thick of Temple Bar foot traffic, the space surrounding An cleared. His nostrils flared with every heated breath and his lips kept twitching, baring clenched teeth. For a moment he caught his reflection and nearly screamed in challenge.

That snapped him out of it. He was no use to Charlie like this.

He wrestled the madness down and strove to ignore the depression that flowed into its place. He moved more methodically through the city with an eye out for the hunter but hoping to find his friend. He believed he caught fleeting glimpses of Jeger, occasionally sensing what might have been the trail of his horn, but An could not be certain. The presence of magic in the city and the crowds muddled his senses. There was enough whiff of Jeger's trail to lead An southward, but not give him a clear sense of direction.

Giving up on the hunter for now, An turned his focus back toward finding Charlie.

Gritting his teeth, he crossed the street toward St. Stephen's Green thinking to search the shadows beneath the trees, where the street kids like to hang after dark. Before he could dodge them, a cluster of women intersected his path. He grunted as he collided with a mass of soft curves and flowing skirts. Bell-like laughter rose in the night as two delicate hands gripped his arms to the musical clatter of a multitude of bangles. More laughter, just as loud and melodious rose around him until An cursed at the attention the bevy surrounding him drew.

"Ah, La-La! What a catch! Toss that one here if you even think of lobbin' him back."

"Now, now, La-La! Don't listen to her... family before all others, yeah, *cousin*?"

The catcalls and ribald comments continued as An sought to extract himself, but he stilled as soon as he recognized the Romani lilt to their voices and took heed of the name they called to.

"La-La?" he asked on a bare breath. He peered into the woman's face, finding familiar dark eyes asparkle among a riot of long, thick curls he knew would be a warm honey brown in the daylight. His hands came up to rest on her shoulders and hope seized his breath, scarcely believing to encounter this one here. She was not alicorn, or even aliman, but she knew him and his kind. Her Clan... the Kalderăs Clan, had oft sheltered members of his herd.

Perhaps... but no, he could not sense any kin among those with her. Still, the Clan might be able to help. They held a magic of their own... for tracking, for Seeing. And they knew Charlie. Cared for her. If anyone could help him find the girl, it was the Rom.

The woman stilled, a frown on her face as she peered closer. He watched her gaze lose focus as her Sight kicked in and she saw beyond his glamour. Her eyes crinkled and her smile grew warmer.

"Lor...!" She started to squeal the name she knew him by, only An darted his hand out and pressed it over her lips, giving a sharp shake of his head. Jeger knew that name, but not the face An wore now to hide his own.

The sparkle in her gaze dimmed as she noticed the changes in him, along with his behavior. She scanned around them for trouble. Her forehead creased as none was evident, but any good Rom knew when best to be silent, and to fade from notice. She gestured to the women she was with. With a nod, they swarmed past the two of them, and moved off, their voices rising higher and more exuberant than before as they danced and laughed and drew everyone's eye off of the two they left behind.

An let La-La claim the hand he'd raised and draw him into the shelter of the boughs overhanging the wrought-iron fence surrounding the park. Together they turned and headed off in the opposite direction, both remaining silent and moving swiftly, once the attention of the masses was firmly anchored on the Romani women now playing "gypsy" to the hilt.

"Talk to me, my friend," La-La said once the crowds had been left behind, gently slipping her hand into the crook of his arm and reining him back to a more leisurely pace as they moved off down a quiet cobbled street. Her calm demeanor conflicted with the worry woven through her scent.

An stopped abruptly. He could not help it.

La-La turned back toward him. The worry blossomed in her gaze as she noted his faint trembling. He flinched when she peered closer at him, her brow furrowed. The muscles of An's face twitched as he tried to answer her, but he could not say the words. Could not tell her of his cleaving. She must have read something in his expression, though, because her hand rose slowly, as if not to startle, and gently brushed beneath the locks hanging heavy across his forehead.

He clenched his eyes shut at the sight of her silent tears as she mourned his loss.

"There is a hunter in the city... Den Jeger," An told her, his voice low and controlled, his tone flat. "He has gone to ground. I am afraid he has taken a friend of mine with him to force my hand."

As he filled the Rom in, fury kindled in her gaze. She reached out and took his hand, striding off with a determined gate.

"Where are we going?"

"Phoenix Park," she murmured. "The others need to know. An' perhaps we can help find... your friend."

As they made their way across the city the crowds lessened as the spaces grew more open. An turned his focus inward toward his meager trickle of magic and allowed La-La to guide him. Centering, he charged his senses and extended them outward, seeking Jeger's trail through the essence of the spire. His spirit surged. As they followed the Liffey toward Phoenix Park the trail strengthened.

La-La tried to draw him toward the Clan's camp, but An tugged his arm out of her grip. His nostrils flared as he caught the faintest trace of Charlie's scent wafting on the breeze. She was here, somewhere. Beyond Phoenix Park. Behind him he heard the electronic tones of a cell phone dialing but ignored it, his stride lengthening as he left La-La behind.

An tracked Jeger to an abandoned warehouse in the Bally-mount Industrial Estate, south of the city, past the park. A fire had left the building a burned-out husk not quite a year ago. The walls were solid, but the roof was gone in patches and the windows altogether. The gaps in the walls had been boarded over, but one had been pried away, left prominently propped against the smoke-scarred wall.

Through with games, An Rógaire stalked up the path between the buildings and straight to the way left open for him. He went alone, unwilling to risk the Rom in this private battle. Though he envied them the promise of death they and all mortals held, he would not be the cause of them embracing that state before they must. They'd trailed him anyway, he could tell by their scent on the air, but for now they hid themselves among the surrounding buildings. It galled him that he could not stop them, but he found it a comfort as well.

As he walked past a bunch of brambles closest to his target, La-La's voice whispered from the brush, "No fear, Lorcan. No matter what happens, the bastard won't walk away from this with your spire." Her vow touched him, as did her insistence on acknowledging his former self, but he could not let that distract him from his purpose.

"Go conquer your demon and when you're done you will return to the Clan so we may heal your hurts. You and your friend."

He shook off her words and kept walking, but nonetheless they warmed his heart. The Kalderăs Clan might not be his own, but their solidarity lent him strength... and hope, misplaced as it was. An Rógaire wasn't really concerned about walking away tonight, as long as Jeger didn't either, but to know Charlie had a place to be safe. He nearly reeled with the relief he felt at that.

La-La must have Sensed his thoughts. She called after him in a low whisper, only loud enough to reach his sensitive ears. "I mean it, Lorcan. There is one who has joined the Clan who might heal even the most grievous of your wounds. You might recognize her name. She is called Anu..."

*Anu?* Surely he had not heard La-La correctly. A healer who bore the name of the Mother Goddess...? Powerful enough to restore him? His chest tightened as he longed to believe.

Forgetting the wisdom of silence, he pivoted to meet La-La's gaze. "What?!"

She nodded, but said nothing, as she drew back into her sheltering spot. He read the belief in her bright eyes before she fluttered her hands at him, shooing him toward the building. He continued forward, burying the seed of hope La-La had planted before it could distract him further.

As he drew closer to the warehouse the stench of old ash and moldering concrete assaulted his senses, overlaid by a heavy odor of industrial chemicals he could not identify either by origin or source. He marveled at the strength of it after all this time.

Huffing out his breath in an effort to clear the scents from his head, An climbed through the gap in the wall only to be assaulted by the odors ten-fold. How could they still be so strong? As he struggled against the overload, he was unsurprised to discover Den Jeger waiting for him. He locked gazes with the hunter and saw a mad glint in the man's eyes. Concerned, An resisted the urge to glance toward Charlie, slumped and bound to a chair in the middle of the vacant warehouse.

"Took you long enough to show up," Jeger said with a sneer. "I thought I'd have to try sheep next if neither girls *nor* boys served to lure you."

For a moment An was puzzled until he realized Jeger thought *Charlie* was a boy. Puzzled enough that he almost missed the insult. An curled his lip in response, but he did not otherwise acknowledge Jeger's barb.

"You have something that is mine," An said, his voice freely channeling his wrath for the first time since the cleaving.

Jeger's hand moved over the ivory spire sheathed at his hip, as if that was all that could possibly matter here. "Come closer, hellspawn. I'd be glad to give it back to you."

An could imagine all too well Jeger's meaning, envisioning his severed horn resheathed in his own chest, as it had once nestled among the ribs of this man's brother. That image haunted An. Alicorn were meant to heal, not harm, yet in his fear and his thrashing An had impaled the mortal intent on harvesting the very horn that ended him. And yet, Jeger's brother had not failed. Already partially hewn away, An's spire had snapped beneath the corpse's weight to become Jeger's trophy.

It would crush Jeger to know the death he dreamt of dealing this day was doomed to fail if the only weapon he'd armed himself with was the spire. The thought almost amused An, until the hunter interrupted.

"Time to pay for my brother's death, beast."

"There is no payment due, the thief owns the risk when he steals what is not his."

Jeger answered him with a rage-filled scream as he drew the spire and lunged forward. An nearly answered him, but Charlie's safety was dependent on An keeping his head. He flowed away from the path of attack with an echo of the grace he'd once had, barely resisting the instinctual urge to reach out and steady the man attacking him. How ironic, were Den Jeger to impale himself. But no, the hunter pivoted and lashed out again, grazing An's arm. In an instant the wound healed, leaving a rent in An's sleeve, and nothing more, not even a crimson stain. The sensation of magic's caress nearly sent An to his knees as the blow itself had not.

"For you?!" Jeger spat, nearly foaming in his rage. "It still works for you?"

It was true. Once one, always one. Severed or not, the one person the spire would always heal was the one it had been cleaved from, of anything short of restoring the cleaved horn itself. Still, An was not about to try and explain the principle of sympathetic magic to his attacker. They were both haunted by the memory of that same horn jutting from the half-healed wound in the chest of Jeger's brother. The moment it broke free from An, it had lost its ability to heal as far as others were concerned.

He shrugged now, knowing it would infuriate the hunter, make him sloppy. "Maybe it was for old time's sake." In a calculated move, An held out his hand, palm up. "Come on, it is useless to you…"

"But not to *you*, which means I am all the more inclined to keep it." Hatred burned in Den Jeger's gaze. "Of course, there is one condition under which I would gladly return it to you." The hunter lunged and thrust once again. Even knowing it would fail to slay him, for an instant An felt the urge to fling his arms wide and bare his chest to Jeger's thrust. Shoving down *that* madness—more his personal demon than Jeger could ever be— An backed away, slowly circling. He focused every effort on drawing the hunter away from Charlie, who had come to and was working free of her bonds. As he carefully made his way through the wreckage left by the fire, fresh bursts of the earlier stench assaulted him. He glanced down and nearly stumbled as his gaze took in darkened concrete and glistening wood. Glancing back up, he saw two things that chilled him: Den Jeger, lost to madness, clutching a newly struck match; and Charlie, creeping up behind the hunter, hand reached out to snatch An's spire.

In that moment, with La-La's words echoing in his memory, An Rógaire... no... *Lorcan* understood he had no more desire for death.

His or anyone else's... not even Den Jeger.

Leaping forward he grabbed for the match.

Startled, Jeger jerked back, his chemical-spattered clothes going up like a torch.

"No..." Lorcan barely murmured, anguish thickening his cry. "Charlie! RUN!"

She didn't hesitate. Even as Jeger shrieked in agony, with the kind of speed only a kid living on the streets possessed, Charlie snatched the spire from the hunter's grasp and shoved off in the other direction. But even she was not fast enough. An heard her hiss as she stopped short.

Already the fire had spread to every puddle and soaked surface until it crackled and snapped and roared at them from all sides. Charlie turned to An, eyes at once both panicked and trusting. He spied a patch of red, angry skin on her cheek where a bit of flame had licked too close. Crouching, coughing, he dove through the flames to reach her. Tucking her beneath the scant protection of his body, Lor searched for some way out.

He searched in vain.

And then he felt it. On his arm, where the spire Charlie still clutched brushed his skin, magic cascaded across his burns, healing them even as falling embers created more.

*Once one, always one.*

Dare he hope? Dare he not?

Unable to talk for the coughing, he reached out and took the spire from her hand and found the raw edge by touch. With a prayer to the Mother Goddess, he lifted the horn to his head, nestled it perfectly in place. Everywhere it touched, it tingled like crazy, but he knew it would not stay, and if it would not stay, this would not work. He could not take his true form and still hold the spire in place, assuming this was even possible at all.

Lorcan gathered his courage and vowed to live.

"Charlie... listen..." he lost his words in another coughing fit as the smoke grew thicker and the heat seized his throat. He shielded his face and tried once more. "Up on my back. Hold this in place and no matter what don't let go." He helped her clamber up as he choked out his commands, trusting she would either listen, or they would die.

She clung to him, trembling and crying silent tears, but with her hand steadfast as she held the spire to its base.

Lor closed his eyes against the sting of chemical-laden smoke and prayed again with every bit of faith he could muster.

The tingle became a burn of a different sort as magic flooded through him and Lorcan instantly transformed, tail flagged and mane thrashing, muzzle long and teeth bared as he challenged death with a defiant scream. Bunching his muscular hindquarters, he charged the flaming beast, his hooves ringing like steel on the concrete as they carried them through the open gap where he'd entered out into the cool night air to land among the Rom, who had swarmed the building and looked ready to charge the blaze.

For a brief instant Lorcan was whole again.

And then he was not, as Charlie slid half-conscious from his singed back. Lorcan collapsed beside her, coughing great hacking coughs as he took on his human seeming once more. But, as he reached out a hand to cradle his dropped spire, Lor did not despair.

Because they were alive, and there was hope.

# The Devil in the Details

THE NAKED LIMBS OF THE GNARLED TREE REACHED HIGH ABOVE Camden Finn as if to snatch the stars from the sky. The night was harsh, the air dry with the extreme cold. All around, snow glittered on the ground... everywhere *except* beneath The Tree.

Camden shuddered and edged back. He was new here in Basking Ridge. The odd kid out; the weirdo. Somehow all the others at school knew he'd been sent to live with his Grandmother Camilla because Mamma wasn't right in the head. Or that's what they said, anyway, before they dared him to touch the cursed tree with a history of hangings... both lawful and otherwise.

Around him, the light breeze grew more forceful until it rattled the branches overhead, making them moan and sigh and wail. Camden shivered again and jerked back further. The sound echoed his last memory of Mamma, both screaming gibberish and sobbing as if her best friend had died, all while being strapped into a strange, white coat. Reaching not for him, but for her favorite oak tree; the one she kept getting caught climbing naked, until the day the ambulance had come to take her away.

Camden couldn't really blame anyone for calling his little family weird. Heck, he'd be the first to admit it. After all, he'd been a part of it for thirteen years.

For nearly half an hour he stood there in the bitter cold, trying to get up the nerve to move closer and touch the bole. He just couldn't do it. Something deep inside him fought the very concept. As if before him lay true madness and to press his skin against it courted such within himself. He was, however, both fascinated and horrified by the chain-link fence wrapped so close around the tree that the bark had begun to swallow it. Beneath the links he could see great, gaping scars from where the superstitious had tried to bring the old tree down.

In the distance, a revving engine broke the spell on him. Camden jumped and spun around, his eyes scanning the road. The other kids had taunted him, telling him a speeding black car would get him, if he drew near the tree. He bet one of them had talked an older sibling into coming out and pranking him if he proved braver than they thought he'd be.

Squaring his shoulders, he turned back to the oak and, before he could talk himself out of it, he lurched forward, slapping his left palm against the bark. Seconds later he yanked it away, overwhelmed by a desperate sense of grasping, of some essence—somehow oddly familiar—clinging to his.

He landed on his ass as he stumbled back, vigorously rubbing his palm down the rough cords of his pants. The skin itched and burned as if little runnels of acid etched its surface. Peering at his hand, he very nearly screamed. For a brief instant in the starlight, it seemed the pattern of the bark had clung there, shaping the skin.

Again, the revving of an engine, followed by the squeal of tires on asphalt.

Camden scrambled to his feet. With teeth chattering and the muscles across his shoulders knotted, he hurried in a limping jog across the field away from the road. Compulsively, he kept looking behind him, almost missing the blaze of the car's headlights as he noticed the brisk wind dancing in his wake, brushing away his footprints.

*Maybe Mamma wasn't the only one going mad*, he thought as he scrambled even faster to reach the trees at the edge of the meadow as the car pursued him.

Camden was back. He couldn't help it. The tree drew him. Called to him... a forsaken soul alone in the meadow. He could identify with it.

There was little to nothing left of the snow, except some dirty, knobby piles sheltered from the sun. Weeks had gone by since he had touched the tree. He'd told the others, but they'd called him a liar. His hand still tingled, but otherwise looked normal, leaving him nothing to show for his daring.

His classmates, led by Antony, the school bully, kept egging him on, demanding he bring them some kind of proof, being too chicken to follow him out here to see for themselves. He couldn't imagine what kind of proof he could bring that they wouldn't just call another lie.

He'd never had a cell phone, a situation his grandmother hadn't bothered to rectify. It hardly mattered, though... he'd yet to psych himself up enough to even cross beneath the tree's branches.

He caught himself rubbing his palm against his leg, something he'd been doing since that first fateful night. The skin still looked like normal skin, if a little rougher and more calloused, only every so often it seemed to shimmer a grey-green shade, like the mossy bark of an oak tree. He had to be imagining it. He'd looked up the legends surrounding the tree and all they mentioned was some crackpot notion that if you touched the tree your hand would turn black if you ate at a diner.

*Who came up with this crazy-ass shit?*

With a final look at his hand, Camden turned and headed home.

Weeks went by. The barest hint of spring had begun to chase away winter's chill. Every time Camden turned around he would swear there was a black car somewhere nearby, windows tinted illegally dark, but then he would look again and it would be gone. He told himself not to be stupid and did his best to forget about the tree and all the legends he'd read about, as his classmates seemed to have done. They taunted and bullied but had apparently lost interest in the challenge they'd issued.

Left to himself, shunned even by the outcasts, Camden spent a lot of time knocking around his grandmother's place, hanging out in the vast yard. Never quite feeling welcome there any more than he did at school.

He began to notice something quite peculiar while striving to stay out of her way. There was no wood. No trees in the yard, no white picket fence. In fact, hers was wrought-iron, beautifully ornate, but cold and hard. Even the house, he learned, was poured concrete, and the garage at the back of the property was a stark, cinderblock building with large metal doors locked tight. He had tried to peer in the dusty windows, but his grandmother came across him poking around. Her gaze, when he caught her eye, was stony as she sharply pointed him away.

Though she generally seemed to ignore him as much as possible—while providing his care within the letter of the law— from that point forward he felt constantly watched.

When he went to sleep that night, he dreamt to the sound of tree branches wailing, dreams that did not bear remembering.

"That's private property you keep skulking around," Grandmother snapped at him one morning, just around the spring equinox. She stood in front of the kitchen sink washing dishes, as stiff as one of her wrought-iron fence rails. "Stay away from that infernal tree. You keep away from that meadow or I'll let the sheriff deal with you."

Camden nodded, but said nothing. He flinched as she whirled on him, grabbing his arm and shaking him. "Do you hear me, young man?"

"Yes, Grandmother," he stuttered, shocked by the strength she wielded, despite her seeming age. This was the first time she had ever touched him.

His grandmother *hmph*ed and turned away, her expression hard and etched with bitterness.

Until they had come for his mother, Camden hadn't even known he had a grandmother. Though she did her duty and took him in, she clearly did not seem at all pleased about it. She was his father's mother, according to the social worker. His father... there was something else Camden had never had, at least not in any practical sense. He had passed away early on, before Camden had been old enough to remember him. Even so, by the stories Mamma had shared, and the love she'd clearly felt, Camden found it hard to believe his father had come from this harsh, unfeeling woman.

He wondered exactly how many days until he turned eighteen and had no one to answer to but the law?

Lowering his head, he pretended interest in his cold breakfast until Grandmother threw down her rag and left the room. That was when he caught himself again rubbing his palm against his leg. He brought his other hand up and ran his fingertip along where the tingling had begun to burn. His palm was rough and thick, but he could feel his veins prominently, branching like roots beneath the skin.

Shuddering, he drew his fingers away, cold chills coursing through him.

Camden dreamt of his mother. Her willowy form, her delicate features, the sense of wildness about her, and the slight edge of madness in her gaze that he had for so long denied the existence of—eased, if not banished, only when she draped herself among the tree branches, bare skin against bark, not quite one with the tree... but longing to be—but most of all he dreamt of her desperately grasping for the branches as she was pulled from it that very last time. Of the panic in her gaze as the strange men restrained her, of the hopelessness that dimmed her gaze while Camden watched the vehicle containing her drive further away.

He woke, gasping, and all he could think of was that damned chain-link fence wrapped around the gnarled oak... so reminiscent of the restrains binding his mother.

Camden could do nothing for her, but the tree... that was different.

Though every impulse screamed at him 'No!,' a wild, crazed idea took root. Quietly, he climbed from bed and drew on his clothes, not bothering with socks or shoes. With gentle steps, he crept to the window and slowly slid the sash open. A firm push popped the screen from the window. Camden grabbed it before it could clatter to the pavers below and leaned it against his bedroom wall before climbing out and sliding the window shut behind him.

In the moonlight, his shoulders itched more than his palm ever did. Ignoring the sensation of being watched, he made his way across town until he came to Antony's house. He knew which bedroom belonged to the bully because he often tossed things at Camden as he was walking by. Not bothering to be quiet, Camden rapped on the glass.

He heard a thud, then watched as the window opened, revealing Antony's scowling face.

"You are so dead, dickwad..."

Camden ignored him. "Give me a bolt cutter and I'll give you the evidence that I touched the tree."

Antony smirked. "Yeah... right."

"Give it to me, or I'll tell everyone you were too much of a pussy to touch the tree yourself."

The expression on the bully's face grew even uglier, at odds with his tousled hair and pajamas. When he came through the open window, Camden braced himself for violence, but the other boy just crept around to the garage and disappeared inside, coming out a moment later with the bolt cutters.

"Have the proof tomorrow, or I'm kicking your ass... and either way, I'm telling my dad you're stealing these..." Antony's father was the sheriff.

Camden just took the tool and turned away, hurrying off into the night in the direction of the meadow—and The Tree.

The moon sat heavy and full in the sky, bathing the meadow in a pale, blue glow seemingly everywhere except in the area surrounded by The Tree. He couldn't help but think of the name he discovered when researching the legends... The Devil's Tree.

He shivered. Though the air of madness surrounding the oak scared the piss out of him, instinct told him the essence of the tree was not evil. Steeling himself, he approached the bole, gaze locked on the angry scars left by frightened mortals, the metal links yet binding and cutting the tree.

Dropping to his knees, he wedged the snipping end of the bolt cutters against the first link, cringing as the steel cut more into the bark than the fence. A sharp pain shot through his left hand, but he continued to leverage his weight on the handles of the tool, half murmuring apologies, though he scarcely knew why, or to whom. With a sharp snap, the first link gave away. He sensed a satisfaction not altogether his own. The meadow seemed poised in anticipation, a hush descending to blanket out the hum of usual night sounds.

As he started on the second, the gunning of a distant engine reached his ears. Straining until pain screamed through his hand, Camden struggled even harder to cut through the links. He was barely three quarters of the way through when bright lights pinned him to the tree. With all his weight he got through all but the last bit of fence before he heard the squeal of brakes behind him and felt the sting of rocks thrown up from the still-hard ground.

"Get away from that tree, you devil spawn!" Venom dripped from the words.

Again, Camden found his grandmother's strength unexpected as she shoved him away from the final link before he had cut all the way through. He managed to keep his grip on the bolt cutters but lost his balance. "You will not release her now! You will not set her free to corrupt more good men like my Tommy!"

Some small part of him noticed the roar of a second car approaching, but most of his focus stayed riveted as he realized the 'devil' his grandmother spoke of was his mother.

She wasn't making sense, but even more than ever, Camden was driven to strip the iron fence from the tree. He eyed the final link, which held together with the barest sliver, so slight he dared wonder if he would even need the bolt cutters to break it free.

His grandmother stood over him, her eyes ablaze and no small measure of madness dancing around the edges of her expression. Camden was certain he spied loathing for him in her gaze. Her chest heaved and outrage etched harder lines into her face than those already there.

"Why did you even take me in?" Camden asked.

"That she-devil stole my only son, but you are half his and by God, I *will* see the demon half run out of you."

She moved forward as if to strike him. Camden set his left hand behind him, bracing for the blow. He gasped as his flesh came down on a gnarled root. Heat blazed through him from the point of contact until he seemed to swell with it, weariness draining from his limbs as strength filled him as it never had before. In the moonlight his skin seemed subtly ridged, like an echo of the oak bark before him, a state that struck him as both strange and fitting, if a puzzle for later. For now, there were other things to deal with.

He did not raise a hand to his grandmother, but he did climb to his feet, flexing his toes in the dirt and grass as he tightened his grip on the bolt cutters.

Tension crackled on the air as she took a step closer, brandishing a crowbar she must have carried from the large, black Cadillac still running behind her.

As she moved, a second car drew up beside the first, strobe lights sending wild pulses of color across the meadow. The door clicked open and the sheriff's voice called out, "Camilla, you will stop right there…"

For a moment, she looked like she would resist, but slowly the tip of the crowbar lowered to the ground. Feeling nothing but pity for the bitter woman who confused love with hate, Camden looked away, meeting the sheriff's gaze.

"This is my land, my tree, my fence! I want him arrested for destroying private property."

"He's your grandson…"

"He's hellspawn!"

Before the sheriff could move to intervene, his grandmother swung the crowbar with all her might. Calm as he had never been calm before, Camden dropped the bolt cutters and raised his right hand to intercept the wicked hook descending on him, the strength of the mighty oak shoring him up. Wrenching the tool from her grip, Camden reversed the hook and yanked with all the power at his disposal on the chain-link fence, snapping the final link and tearing the overgrown fence from the trunk of the tree, sending bark flying.

Grandmother screamed a piercing scream, tearing at her hair as she fell to her knees. As she did so, a surge of power swept through the meadow. Grasses plastered to the ground and the new-minted leaves of the oak tree danced in the moonlight as Camden lifted his eyes to the oak's gnarled crown to recognize the essence of his mother lounging in the upper branches, finally as one with her own her true tree.

# A Moment Out of Time

S ERGEANT JAMES ISAAC STOOD GUARD AT THE PERIMETER OF THE disturbance, his stance steady, though a cold sweat beaded on his dark skin. In front of him, a growing crowd muttered and surged forward as it absorbed more gawkers. He avoided their eyes so he didn't have to see the edge of panic and fear in their gazes. Even so, he kept alert for sudden movements.

Some in the crowd moaned that this was the end of the world. Others waved signs blaming the occurrences on the government or aliens or some super-secret terrorist weapon.

Jim didn't want to see the individual turmoil, didn't want to risk getting sucked into their panic. He trailed his gaze over the crowd watching for trouble. Plenty of people had gone over the edge the last few days, quietly or otherwise; others just tucked their heads down and tried to tell themselves things would get back to normal soon. He wasn't worried about them.

A few... a very few... got a gleam in their eye as they pondered 'what if.'

Those were the dangerous ones.

The ones looking past the horror and danger of what had occurred to plan how they might exploit the situation, for good or evil intent.

Didn't seem they had any of those here today, but Jim kept his guard up and tried not to let his childhood memories flood over him. Though he faced the crowd, in his mind, he could still see the '67 Chevy Impala everyone was staring at, a huge chunk of the front end missing, looking like it had been scooped out neat and clean as a cross-section for some museum display. He heard the owner behind him raising hell at Jim's CO, stridently demanding that they find out who had done this impossible thing. And who would pay for the damages.

Jim could tell him it wasn't impossible at all... just damned inexplicable.

A shudder traveled across his shoulders. He shoved away a decades' old flashback of something infinitely more precious than an antique car just as neatly bisected.

By the time the military transports came to whisk the troops away, along with the remains of the car, Jim sighed, heavy with exhaustion, more from holding off his own demons than any crowd control. He scrambled into the back of the open-framed truck and pulled his cap down over his eyes, settling back for the short hop to the municipal building serving as a temporary barracks. Once there, he ignored the chow line and headed for the workout room to wear himself out in a bid for some dreamless sleep.

As beat as he was after working out, sleep wouldn't come once he hit his bunk. He just couldn't shut down. Instead, he groaned, rolled over until he lay flat, ignoring the answering groan from the army surplus cot beneath him... focusing, instead, on the scratch of stretched canvas on his bare legs and the press of aluminum supports against the small of his back. With a little effort, he could imagine he lay on his sister's poor excuse for a futon.

He almost succeeded. *Almost.*

But there was no ignoring the musty odor clinging to him after just a few restless hours in the makeshift barracks, or the snores of his friend, Private Kyle Donovan, asleep on the next cot.

Opening his eyes, Jim raised a hand to wipe away the sweat clinging to his skin. That was as far as he got toward getting up. He lay there in his military-issue tee shirt and boxers staring at the acoustic-tile ceiling far overhead. Dimples meant to improve their sound-dampening effect pock-marked the putty-white surfaces. Some of the micro-craters were as large as a pencil's eraser, while others were the size of the point. The white areas between varied as much as the indents they surrounded.

One side of Jim's mouth rucked up higher than the other; not exactly a smirk, but by no means half a smile either. That ceiling could represent the city of San Angelo in microcosm: craters had started to appear in the landscape, like someone took out whole bits of it, then dropped other bits in. No one had noticed at first. The effects had been subtle. New-looking brick along part of an old building, a fresh playbill stuck to a wall from a theatre long gone; things that blended into the landscape of an old, midsized city, where people tended not to look too closely at their surroundings, even when they weren't rushing their lives away.

And then things changed.

A little bit of desert—complete with barrel cactus and a nest of scorpions—ended up in a socialite's living room. Three-hundred pounds of brick and mortar materialized in the middle of the newly completed McCormick Boulevard, hanging in mid-air for an instant before crumbling to the blacktop in front of a semi. The driver of the rig went right over the rubble... the Connellys in the car behind, not so much.

Things got more and more interesting from there. Lives disrupted... some lost, and a lot of weirdness kept happening ever since.

People panicked; the police weren't equipped to deal with something on this scale, and, frankly, there weren't enough of them to even try. That was why the armed forces had been called in, mostly newly graduated cadets, raw recruits, reservists, and reactivated veterans, Jim being one of the later. No one had declared martial law, but they might as well have.

Setting those thoughts aside, Jim hauled himself upright and swung his legs down to the floor. His right knee gave a half-hearted throb—a souvenir from the Saudi Desert—and then settled into a familiar dull ache. The rest of him... well, it wasn't like how he felt made a difference to him; as long as his blood was on the right side of his skin and he could stand upright for a reasonable amount of time, he was needed.

It felt good to be needed.

"Yo, Jimbo..."

Jim stared at the young Asian-American kid leaning half through the doorway. How David Koto made second lieuie with that kind of demeanor was a mystery. That brand of informality had to cause him problems with the men under his command. Anyway, it wasn't like it was Jim's problem. He was no longer career military; once this situation was resolved, he'd be back sleeping on his sister's futon while he tried to find a job. He ignored the officer's lax attitude, running a hand over the short, black nap of his hair and encountering the remnants of cold sweat from earlier.

Jim straightened. "Yes, sir?"

"Gather your team and head over to Swanson Street," Lieutenant Koto said. "We have a potential riot situation with the locals."

The cold sweat returned, along with the grim recollection of the last time he'd been to that neighborhood. He shut that memory down and focused on his superior's words.

What the hell... the *locals*? Though he hadn't been back in about twenty years, Jim had grown up on the next street over from Swanson. Likely some of these "locals" were people he knew. Koto made it sound like they were in Iraq or something dealing with insurgents. These were American citizens he was talking about; scared people with no idea how to stay safe from craters no one had figured out how to spot coming.

*This friggin' butter-bar's gonna cause an incident,* Jim thought, *gonna get someone hurt... or killed...* Jim reined back his disgust and carefully schooled his expression back to neutral. Kid probably didn't even know the Saudi Desert from the beach. But it wasn't Jim Isaac's place to instruct him.

"Yes, sir. Right away, sir," he replied. His gut clenched into a tightly wound coil, which he doggedly ignored.

He didn't know why he'd bothered to respond at all. Koto was already out the door.

Leaning over, Jim hauled out his kit and hefted it onto the cot. After he pulled on his pants, he took his mini tablet out of his pack and slid it into one of his many cargo pockets before checking over his pistol, and then his rifle, then standing up to strap on his field gear. When he finished, he tugged on his billed cap and leaned over Donovan to give his shoulder a shake.

"Come on, soldier. Grab your gear," Jim ordered. "We have to go do damage control."

As he left the room, he rubbed the fingers of his right hand, a childhood habit that cropped up once in a while. He tensed even more as he felt the gap where the tip of his middle finger used to be.

He had lost it on Swanson Street.

Coffee cups and scribbled notes littered Dr. Yoseph Cohen's workbench, along with drips of solder, snippets of wire, and tossed-aside circuit boards. In sharp contrast, well-used tools lay in precise formation mere inches from his hand, awaiting service.

Yoseph pushed aside the clutter to uncover the machinery beneath. His fingers trembled slightly as he reached for the control panel linked to the massive machine swallowing most of the space of his modest workroom. Noting the tremors, he fisted his hand to still them. His gaze drifted to the dollar-store picture frame propped beside his state-of-the-art computer, the faux gilding worn away on one side from handling. His wife's gaze caught his own, her lively mischief nearly captured for all time in the bright glint in her eye, and the promise of a smile not quite flourished upon her lips. Yoseph groaned with the heartache represented by that photograph, taken mere days before he lost her right here in the lab, the accident so sudden he had been powerless to stop it. His Kitya... gone almost twenty years.

Their son would have been nineteen this day if she had lived to bear him.

"This time," he murmured, flipping and reflipping switches to ensure that the mechanism was properly engaged. He moved toward the machine dominating the room like something out of an etching from a first-edition novel by Jules Verne. Round, like a riveted ball, it had four portholes evenly spaced around its ten-foot circumference and ornate brasswork everywhere else.

A ring circled the base and gave the machine the appearance of a peculiar Faberge ostrich egg on a short pedestal. Yoseph checked the sensors and gauges dotting the surface with methodical precision. The reddish tint of the aged glass caps lent the workshop a rosy glow as the sensors lit up. Kitya had loved the Victorian esthetic that had made his great-great grand-father's invention as much a work of art as of science. For her sake, Yoseph had strived to preserve as much of the ornamentation as possible. The inner workings, however, had been gutted and reworked countless times since his great-great grandfather—for whom Yoseph had been named—had first assembled the housing. And, after the fire, not one circuit or wire was original.

Yoseph would have walked away from his family's legacy after his wife's death, only it was his sole hope of saving her. Somewhere in their research, he had to find the key. Thanks to the first Yoseph's vision and those who had come later, the study and manipulation of time filled a whole library of journals housed in the alcove just off the laboratory. Many of the books were stained and crumbling from age and long use, others were virgin yet, waiting their turn to document this Yoseph's findings.

He had lost any interest in painstaking documentation after his wife's death. Now all he cared for were results.

Drawing a deep, centering breath, he ignored the heavy weight at the middle of his chest and initiated the start-up procedure before swinging open one segment of the sphere and climbing inside.

His head spun, and his vision pulled reality out of shape like taffy as the mechanism clicked and clacked away. Yoseph struggled to remain alert but lost the battle.

Jim had a hard time keeping his cool once his team reached Swanson Street. The memories of the last time he'd been there kept swarmed up no matter how hard he tried to lock them down. His first sight of those milling about didn't help. Other than the clothing styles and the nicer landscaping, he could have been looking back on a day he knew happened twenty years ago.

Lieutenant Koto hadn't been exaggerating about the near riot. What had to be every resident of the neighborhood clustered around a lot that had been converted to a memorial park back when Jim had been just a kid. Tears, outrage, and fear marked many of the faces that turned toward the new arrivals, and from somewhere deep in the pack, more than one woman's voice wailed.

Taking care to move in a non-threatening manner, nine soldiers piled out of the transport and stood waiting for orders. Setting his jaw, Jim climbed from the driver's seat. He slung his rifle across his back but kept his hand near his pistol as he approached those gathered. With his other hand, he motioned for his men to remain where they were and do the same.

"Excuse me," he said in a calm, even tone. "I'm going to need you to step clear and return to your homes."

The crowd turned nearly as one at his words, some with teeth clenched and brows lowered, others with tears streaming down their faces unchecked. Jim noted those with their hands fisted or who seemed to be reaching for concealed weapons. He set his expression in what his unit had called his war face, which scared most of *them* shitless. With legs braced and hard eyes staring from the sharp plains of his face, he pinned each of the potential troublemakers with a steady gaze, allowing the shadow of his combat experience to show through. The armor slipped as an elderly woman caught his eye.

"Jimmy? Little Jimmy Isaac? That you?" Miss Matilda, the woman who mothered half the neighborhood, let loose a broad smile and came forward. "It is, isn't it? I'd know you anywhere, boy. Where's my hug?" The tension hanging over all of them broke as everyone there laughed, if only briefly.

Jim had to smile back. He opened his arms, and she moved right in, leaving a dry kiss on his cheek before stepping back. Slowly, as if taking their cue from their matriarch, the crowd separated, revealing a scene that echoed one of his too-persistent flashbacks, but no one walked away.

If not for his training, Jim would have swayed as his vision hazed over. The memory he'd been fighting overtook him.

Twenty years ago, half a little girl's body had been discovered here in what then had been a vacant lot. The other half was never found.

Until now.

Jim and his friends were the ones to find the remains the first time. They'd come across the body on their way to play stickball. He and Nunez had been shoving each other over something. Jim had stumbled as a sudden wave of intense cold swept across him, biting sharp at the very edge of his out-flung hand. Nunez had tried to catch him but wasn't quick enough. Jim landed right beside what was left of the body. It had been his first eye-to-eye with death.

Literally.

Rosa had been the younger sister of Jim's friend, Sita. No one could explain what happened to her, or how, but Jim had been so freaked out he hadn't realized his own injury until after. There was no blood, anywhere—his or Rosa's—but somehow, the tip of his finger had been sliced away along with half the nail.

Jim heard his men shift subtly behind him, drawing him from the memory. The faintest of tremors skittered across his shoulders. The closer he drew to the site of the incident, the more his skin tingled. He ignored the sensation. There was a job to do and respects to be paid.

In the gap left when the crowd stepped back was a sight that could have been recreated from Jimmy's nightmares. A woman very reminiscent of Rosa's mother crouched beside the grim remains. As Jim moved closer, even the chill of the air seemed transported across the intervening years until he nearly shook with it, if not for the rigid control that had been trained into him.

Drawing his cap from his head, he knelt on one knee beside the young woman muttering and wailing in a hodge-podge of Spanish and English. With the lightest of touches, he rested his hand on her shoulder and bowed his head briefly, ignoring the gasps and grumbles at his back. When he looked up, the woman... *Sita...* stared back at him.

On the ground before her lay the missing half of Rosa's body, looking as if twenty years hadn't passed. Understandably, Sita appeared shocked. He watched her struggle to cope with this fresh horror resurrected from their youth.

"I don't understand," Sita moaned as she clutched her dead sister's hand.

"None of us do," Jim answered as he wrapped his arm around her before loosening her grip on the body and helping her up. He found a sense of closure as, for a brief moment, she leaned into his hold before Miss Matilda and a bevy of neighborhood women drew Sita away. Head still bowed; Jim remained motionless as he murmured a prayer for the family of this young soul lost between times.

Before the grumbling could climb to a clamor, Jim turned slowly, addressing the throng, keeping his tone firm but nonaggressive. "Unless you are family, please return to your homes." Surprisingly, they complied. Jim then turned to Donovan. "Get on the radio and call in for a clean-up."

As the private went to do as ordered, Jim pulled out his tablet and documented the scene, taking notes and getting pictures of the body and its surroundings. At first, nothing seemed out of order—other than the remains—but then Jim knelt again and fingered the ground and the trampled greenery. He shuddered once before he got control of himself and continued his inspection. For about ten feet around, the ground was mostly clay and full of rocks, instead of the rich loam that made up the surrounding landscape. Likewise, the plants seemed more typical of a vacant lot, not a maintained park. The severed edge of the body hugged the perimeter of this zone, and as Jim finished his inspection, he gasped and felt the blood drain from his face. He barely heard when footsteps came up behind him as he crouched there unmoving.

"Hey, Sarge, what is it?"

Getting control of himself, Jim took a picture of the ground before him, where a tiny bit of brown flesh still connected to half a nail lay as equally preserved as Rosa.

"Nothing," he murmured as he pulled a handkerchief from his pocket and folded the missing bit of his finger inside.

Heat woke Yoseph. Intense heat, like he sat within the fringes of a bonfire. He jerked upright against the restraints holding him in the central seat of the travel pod. His gaze darted around the compartment.

Reality had returned to its normal consistency, but heat still tormented his flesh, edging his motions with panic. The straps resisted as he yanked at them. Or perhaps his fingers merely fumbled as anxiety fractured his focus, and the harsh sound of his breathing sawed against his ears.

It took a moment—and the absence of flames engulfing him—for Yoseph to calm. Even then, he ran still-trembling hands over his limbs and body looking for burns, too overwhelmed by the memories of his wife's death in this very pod to believe that fire did not lick at him. Exhaustion eroded his usually impenetrable mental barricade. Twenty years fell away in seconds, though not in the manner he had intended, as the images of her death pierced through his defenses. He had not heard her screams in time, muffled as they had been by the pod's thick walls. By the time he'd seen the flicker of the flame inside, it had been too late. Yoseph had watched Kitya burn, unable to get the external safety latch open in time to save her.

Finally managing to disengage his restraints, Yoseph fled the restored pod and slammed the hatch closed behind him. He struggled to control his breathing as he scanned his workshop, searching for some sign of change that would tell him this recent test had not been a failure.

Nothing.

He gritted his teeth and brought his fist down on his desk. More time wasted. Another day his beloved remained dead. Ashamed, he could not look upon her photograph as he shut down the control panel. As he did so, a phantom tang of burning ozone haunted him. Memory or further mishap? He could not say. All the alarms he had installed after his wife's death had remained silent. No smoke, no hot spots in the circuitry. Even so, this evening would be spent manually inspecting every inch of the machine's interior. Once he rescued Kitya, it could burn until the metal formed a puddle on the ground for all he cared, but not until then.

"What are we doing here again?"

Jim did not respond. He barely heard Donovan. The wall before them held Jim's full attention. This location was one of the first documented time bubble sites; though no one had recognized it as such at first. He worried his lip as he continued to study the patch of seemingly new bricks out of place among their age-weathered cousins, some seamlessly bisected like those before-and-after shots that helped keep Photoshop jockeys employed. An autumn breeze fluttered the remnants of the playbill, which someone had ripped away. A frown ridged Jim's forehead as he looked from the wall down to the picture displayed on his tablet. The circle looked smaller, but how could that be? Leaning closer to the wall, Jim lightly touched a finger to the demarcation point.

"Yo, dude," Donovan tried again.

"It's fading."

Everywhere his finger touched, the older-looking bricks lightly crumbled. When he rubbed the tips of his fingers together, they tingled where the dust coated them, and his hand felt chilled. Quickly, he brushed the stuff off before he learned the hard way what affect it might have.

Raising his tablet, he opened the camera app and snapped a fresh photo of the wall.

"Come on," Donovan shoved his shoulder. "This is supposed to be a lunch run... not a site-seeing tour."

"Aren't you curious, man?"

"I'm hungry," Donovan said as he tugged on Jim's arm. "I'm *curious* when I'm gonna get to eat."

Jim laughed and pulled free. "Yeah, whatever." He slipped the tablet into his thigh pocket, and they headed off down the street.

They were a block away, heading toward Lieutenant Koto's favorite sandwich shop, when Jim started to tense. He rolled his shoulders, trying to shake the sensation, but it only grew worse as they moved further from the site of the time bubble. He turned to say something to Donovan when he felt a tingle grow to his left, where the private kept pace with him. A sudden wave of chilled air followed.

"Sonofa*bitch!*" Jim reached out and yanked Donovan toward him, sending both of them to the pavement. When he looked up, he saw a piece of a heavy metal garbage bin materialize and crash to the ground inches from Donovan's foot.

"What the hell?" Donovan murmured beside him. "Who threw that?"

Jim didn't correct him, but he did pull his tablet from his cargo pocket and start snapping shots of this newest time bubble, all the while trying not to think on how his friend had almost ended up like Rosa.

The glow of Jim's laptop lit the room like the tail end of twilight. He'd lowered the brightness on the monitor as dim as it would go, though he knew most of his fellow soldiers could sleep with no problem even in the full light of day. Still, he didn't want to draw attention to what he was doing. Early on in the situation, he suggested to Koto that they track the incidents and figure out what was going on to be proactive instead of reactive.

The lieutenant had blown him off, saying their job was to control the situation while others figured out what was going on.

Asshole.

Jim had not argued—what good soldier would?—but he had brought it up again today after the time bubble incident. Koto laughed, clearly not believing Jim had any way of sensing an incident. The lieutenant still would not budge and allow the teams to officially gather data, but as he had not ordered otherwise, there was nothing stopping Jim from trying to figure things out on his own time. He had already started documenting incidents out of curiosity and had amassed quite a bit of data with the help of his buddies from other teams. None of the intel made any sense yet, but Jim had only been futzing around with it until now.

Time to get serious. Today had scared the shit out of him, especially after they got back to their makeshift HQ. When they all sat down to eat, Jim had noticed a chunk missing from the sole of Donovan's boot. That had killed Jim's appetite right there. If he had moved even a second slower, it could have been Donovan himself with bits missing.

Jim had spent the evening mapping out the known occurrences on a diagram of the city. The results were not much. The beginning of an imperfect pattern formed with more gaps than points. Jim itched to get out there and take an eyes-on look at those areas where he expected an incident may have been overlooked. Until today, he hadn't realized his childhood experience had left him sensitive to these occurrences. Perhaps that sensitivity might help him identify where a time bubble had already appeared. None of them got much downtime, though. Getting out to canvas the city was going to be tricky. For now, Jim poured over the photos he and others had gathered, trying to pick out what intel he could.

No matter how he braced himself, the images that scrolled across his screen hit him like the bogeyman appearing out of nowhere. For years after they had discovered Rosa's remains, the memory had haunted him, never fading, never dulling. He had learned to deal with it, but this was like a whole new mind trip. Of course, now it did not paralyze him as it had when he was a child. No. This time it galvanized him. He would find who—or what—was responsible and make sure there were no more Rosas to mourn.

"Hey, Isaac… you plannin' on sleepin' any time soon?" Donovan grumbled from the cot beside him. Grimacing to himself, Jim powered down his system and lay back on his cot with nothing but his ghosts to occupy him.

Yoseph had to get her back. He had to try. Nothing else mattered.

Even if he couldn't stop it… he could say goodbye…

They had never let him say goodbye. Jewish law forbade it. Cohens, descended from the high priests of Israel, could not be in the presence of the dead, the unclean. They must remain pure.

Deep in his heart, though, Yoseph was determined. If nothing else, he would say goodbye to his wife, his love… perhaps… he might even join her.

It had taken weeks, and several more deaths, before Jim had enough data to isolate a search zone. Guilt weighed on him at that, but San Angelo was not some small town, and gaining access to private locations had been problematic. Jim's knee ached pretty much constantly from all his roaming.

Once he had an idea of where to look, he had researched the buildings in the zone and those who resided there. He was pretty certain his theory was sound. In the morning, he would go to Koto… or over him. Someone needed to see his findings so they could do something about this.

Not only were people at risk from these occurrences, but Jim had discovered something.

Each time reality reset itself, as it inevitably did, it crumbled a little more.

Though impatient, Yoseph painstakingly made his calculations. He figured out his problem... his mistake. He kept trying to ride the machine to the past, but in the compartment is where Kitya had died. What if his presence there created a paradox preventing his success? This time he would activate the mechanism unmanned. Clearing everything away, sweeping crumpled papers and such to the floor, he input the settings again. Then, with the barest of hesitation, he reached for the switch. Before he could engage the machine, the door to the workroom burst open.

Yoseph jerked around and watched in shock as soldiers poured into the room with weapons raised. They situated themselves around the space as a black man limped forward, gun in his hand but lowered.

"I need you to step away from the machine, Dr. Cohen," Jim ordered as he took up position in front of the man, one Dr. Yoseph Ian Cohen, the Fourth, according to city records, a man who had both a family and a personal history for experimenting with the theory of time travel. And a reason to keep trying.

"All I want is to go back..."

"You can't," Jim told the man, his tone low and even, body braced to react if needed. "It doesn't work that way."

At his words, the man's gaze snapped into focus, and his body went rigid as he pinned Jim with an indignant glare. "How can you possibly know how it works? What do *you* know about any of this?"

The man stepped forward in agitation. At Jim's back came the sound of a soldier charging his weapon. He made a gesture for his team to hold fire. If they were to have any hope of halting the time degradation, they needed this man alive.

"You have no idea how any of this works! You haven't been here. You haven't poured over these journals! You have no grasp of advanced temporal physics!" With each pronouncement, Dr. Cohen grew more agitated until Jim could smell his acrid sweat on the air as his spittle struck Jim's face.

"No, I can't say I do," Jim answered, struggling to maintain his calm demeanor. "But I sure as hell can see the results. I know what it's doing to the city. Every time you turn on that machine, you're playing roulette with people's lives! It's like you're tugging on the fabric of time. You get a grip on a thread and pull it out of place without realizing what you're doing."

As he spoke, Cohen kept shaking his head, denial etching his features at Jim's claims, his eyes more crazed with each second.

Jim lost his cool. "Dammit, man! People have died!"

"Kitya," Cohen murmured in a broken voice.

"Yes, Kitya," Jim responded, having learned about Cohen's wife—and her ill-fated participation in her husband's studies. "But that was an accident, a malfunction. Rosa Ponce, the Connellys, who knows how many others... they died because you keep messing with things even you don't understand."

Cohen looked even more confused; only this time, it was not the disassociated-with-reality type.

"You don't know..." Jim said, hearing the shock in his own voice. Taking a gamble, he slowly holstered his weapon and drew out his ever-present tablet. His muscles tensed at the risk he was taking, but how else could he explain? How else could he get through to this man?

A few taps on the screen brought up the photo gallery. A few more brought up the incident map Jim had constructed, each occurrence radiating out from this location like spray from a bullet wound, dense near the point of entry, sparser further out.

Holding his breath, Jim presented the tablet to the man responsible, watching as Dr. Cohen took it from him and with a swipe of his finger flipped through the images. When the man reached the photos of Rosa, he blanched, his eyes widening. He nearly dropped the tablet, only Jim was ready for it and reclaimed it as the man's grip loosened.

"No..." Dr. Cohen said, his tormented gaze turning to Jim, silently begging, though for what Jim could not say.

"Would your Kitya have wanted this?"

Shame darkened Dr. Cohen's expression, bleeding the life from his gaze. Jim could not begin to imagine being told he was the cause of such tragedy. He worried about the doctor's reaction. They could not afford for guilt to shut the man down, not when he was the only one with any understanding of what he had done. "You can help make it right, sir."

Cohen looked puzzled. "How?"

"Now that we've figured out what's happened, it's time to fix what's broke. We're going to need your help with that."

Strength and purpose returned to Cohen's expression, and Jim could practically see the man's mind turn with full focus toward the problem. Jim knew another moment of unease.

Dr. Cohen had a gleam in his eye as he pondered 'what if.'

# Forever And A Day

"A dream is a memory of what the future may hold if you dare to reach for it."

DESPITE THE CENTURIES THAT HAD PASSED, TALA ATH COULD SEE the image over and over like a flare burning against the lids of her closed eyes. The final ship at lift-off, rocket thrusters scorching the earth beneath with a fire that seemed to rival that of the distant sun. The vessel had been ancient but determined, resurrected for a final chance at glory by the last lingering remnants of the human race on Mother Earth. But for a few thousand scattered souls who with time passed on, mankind had departed for the heavens.

*"Let the fools go."* Declan's long-ago scorn echoed in Tala's mind in time with the vision. *"The Daoine Maith will dance in celebration at their leave-taking."*

Tala's teeth clenched down upon the memory of her friend, cutting it off.

*Talk about fools,* she thought. *There are none so blind as those who will not see.* But oh, the horror in Declan's proud fae eyes when the truth came clear.

At first the Earth had rallied, unfettered by the burden of humanity's disregard, freed from the bounds of pollution. For a time, nature came again into its own as any soul would when a poison is drawn away. Around the world flora and fauna both crept back from the edge of extinction, reclaiming the planet. Tala and her people rejoiced. Everywhere flourished such beauty as had not been seen outside the fae lands since before the advent of humanity. But eventually, in the early days of the Earth's second century without man, the first effects were felt, gradual but persistent. At first things just leveled out, barely enough for any to notice. But then it could not be denied that fewer young were born among Earth's creatures with each generation that passed and less fruit and flowers came from nature's bounty, until even the fae in their sheltered Lands sensed the lessening of all things.

In the absence of mankind's fleeting vibrancy... their passion... the spark that set them apart from all other of Earth's children, nature seemed divest of its sense of purpose. Without the humans' life force and the mage energy sloughed off from them like skin to dust—vital to the ecological balance—those left behind faded. The animals, the plants, and even the fae, though many decades passed before any acknowledged the cause. Declan had been among the first. Though not truly dead, he and others like him drifted into a stupor state from which none woke.

It could no longer be denied: Without humanity, the Earth and all it held were doomed.

With a frustrated huff, Tala turned away from the remnants of the ancient launch pad. Careful steps led her through the crumbling infrastructure of what she was told used to be the Kennedy Space Center. Over the remains of ivy-draped concrete blocks and steel supports rusted through until they appeared like lace, across the memory of long-gone tarmac and past where a stray shard of glass somehow clung to its twisted aluminum frame, Tala's darting gaze sought out the odd jay nesting in crumbling rafters and faded blossoms long-reverted to their wild state rooted in the rich loam of rotted timbers. Her fae heart cringed at the faint yellow cast to the grasses over which she now trod. It had taken centuries, but like a field sown season after season with the same crop, something vital was missing from the Earth and everything that grew upon it.

The planet had lost a piece of its soul and heaven help them all if it could not be gotten back.

Tala continued on her way before the ache grew too much to bear. As she did so a trill gave her faint warning to brace before a small, compact form collided with her calves and took her to the ground.

"Beag Scath!" she scolded but with little heat. She found it difficult not to smile as the sprite wove his head fetchingly, sending his tousle of multi-hued locks bobbing. He grinned and scampered up her limbs to perch by her shoulder.

"Now, what are ye on about?" she asked, meeting the little one's orange gaze. He fussed and didn't speak, but then he seldom did. He was an odd one, bold and brash and long-beloved, having attached himself to Tala's Clan centuries before. Originally companion to the Sidhe who'd called herself Maggie McCormick, he'd glommed on to Tala's grandmother when she first became Maggie's charge and protégé. That was during the ancient days in New York, when Maggie served as both pawnbroker and one of the guardians of that city. Or so Tala had been told in many a bedtime tale.

As if in reaction to her thoughts, Beag Scath reached out with a minute hand to clutch her ear while he leaned forward and brushed a kiss across her forehead.

Suspecting the wee one had not just capriciously bowled her over, Tala closed her eyes and reached out with her thoughts. *Mamó, did ye tell the little monster to dump me on my ass, or was that his idea?*

A dry chuckle and a thread of music teased her inner ear before her grandmother responded from somewhere behind her. "Sorry, *lhiannon*, he got away from me."

Tala tilted her head back to spy her grandmother, Kara-Anu, looking as youthful as Tala herself, with bright amber eyes and a mane of deep red hair curling around and past her shoulders. The case holding her enchanted violin, Quicksilver, hung by its strap across her back, half hidden by those wild tresses. The grin on her grandmother's face woke an answering one on Tala's. "Hi, Mamó."

"Hi yourself. Now up with you, my child, we haven't time for lying about."

Her brow wrinkled in confusion, as Tala clambered to her feet. She had to scramble to keep up with her grandmother, who immediately set out across the clearing back toward the remnants of the launch pad.

"The memory of this place is strong even now," Mamó said as Tala came up beside her. "It might just do."

"Do for what?"

"You've cousins among the Kalderaš Clan... it's time you met them."

Kalderaš! The gypsies. The first to venture forth from the Earth; driven to the stars by prejudice and their race's curse to wander. Tala had grown up on tales of the courtship between the steadfast Jacko and his Sidhe bride, Agnieszka, of the torment of Tony DeLocosta (possessed by an evil demigod and nearly lost in that one's banishing), and endless stories both bright and dark of their children and their children's children. She had never met even one of them, born only after the Rom had journeyed to the stars. Her heart thrilled at the thought of meeting cousins born from those cherished figures. "How?" she asked, turning eager eyes upon her grandmother.

"Come," Mamó beckoned. "It's time to build new dreams out of the old." And she showed Tala her vision as only the Sidhe could. Of the wandering gypsy race finally gaining a home, of the Earth revitalized with the return of her wayward children. Of the world and all it held growing hale and whole and healthy once more. Tala's breath left her in a rush through open lips and her eyes went wide in awe. But without question she followed. This would not be the first time Mamó had saved the world, though few but the fae knew the truth of that other tale. Tala had grown up expecting wonders of Kara-Anu, the mortal girl who had become both fae and goddess.

In the center of the crumbling launch pad, crowded by the memories of long-ago dreams, Tala watched as Mamó cradled Quicksilver beneath her chin and brandished her bow. And then bow arm stroked and fingers danced until Kara-Anu's whole body moved with the power of the song. Tala's spirit calmed until she found herself first humming, then singing, drawn into the spellcasting. Melody and harmony wove about them in a dance of color and light and music such as the world had long done without. The air crackled with the gathering magic. Tendrils and sparks lit up the space surrounding them, music wrapped them in its grip with silky smooth notes that ran like fingers over their hair, raising the strands like burning clouds about their heads. Raw energy ready to do their bidding.

Together they wove a vessel of starlight and moonbeams, of sunshine and life force, powered it with resolve and bound it all tight with their will until before them rested a glittering orb stretched oblong like a grain of fat rice. A touch to the shimmering skin sent rainbow ripples across its surface. Those ripples murmured an echo of the melody woven into the craft's making.

Tala released a quavering breath. What a glorious thing.

"Are you ready, Tala?" her grandmother asked. There was a faintness to her voice that made Tala frown, but she nodded. Mamó ran her fingers along the edge of the orb, folding away a section of the skin. She held out her hand. For a brief moment, Tala could not bring herself to take it, but this was her grandmother, the undying Kara-Anu, sister to the Mother Goddess Danu herself.

Tala allowed her grandmother to aid her into the vessel of light and life. It cradled her as she had not been since she was a child small enough to fit in her Mamó's arms. Tension melted away in the warmth of that embrace. She looked around for Beag Scath, wanting to say farewell, but the sprite was oddly absent, though Tala swore she could faintly hear his cooing. With a frown, she turned her attention back to her grandmother. From where she stood outside, Mamó caressed the orb. "This will get you where you need to be." She paused to draw a cord from around her neck. From it dangled a familiar copper pendant etched with faint runes. "And this will guide you."

The medallion... it was an ancient charm that in ages past had linked a younger Kara to the gypsies before they were kin. It had been given to Mamó by one called Granddame Rose, grandmother to the demigod-possessed Tony. As it settled over her head, Tala sensed the kernel of power still nestled in those runes just as binding as the day they'd first been etched. If tears glistened in her eyes at that gift, her jaw dropped at what came next.

"And she will keep you safe," Kara-Anu decreed with a hard edge of command backing the words as she slipped Quicksilver and her bow into its case, and the case into the space by Tala's feet.

Tala did not argue, but she did ask, "The Kalderaš, what am I to tell them?"

Kara-Anu remain silent a moment her eyes glimmering as she leaned forward, pressing a kiss to Tala's forehead. "Tell them... It's time to come home."

# CROSSROADS AND CURSES



Sound advice... not what I'd expected, but sound just the same—even for someone like me with no belief in witches.

"No need to smirk, human," the elvin warrior grumbled.

I was pretty sure I wasn't but didn't argue. That might piss *him* off and then all of this would have been for nothing. Instead, I examined him closely. If the season were closer to All Hallow's Eve I would expect I was being had. How else to explain a seven-foot-tall, ancient-seeming warrior suddenly sprawled across a rough, old bench in the middle of nowhere?

Only this was Beltane by the pagan calendar, and I'd told no one what I'd intended. Over weeks and months I had gathered those items I'd felt I would need to ensure success. Not one thing I'd brought or worn had been manufactured by modern means, there was no steel or iron anywhere on me, and the burlap sack at my feet contained every protective or ritual object I could possibly need gleaned from the collective legends of the crossroads: twenty-one pennies, three candies; a hazel switch broom; garlic, even a battered violin, and the list went on.

I hadn't needed any of them. Dude must have been bored.

I would swear I'd never seen him before, yet something about him echoed familiar on a subconscious level. With a reporter's trained eye, I took mental note of his long, narrow features. His tabard—worn over a heavy tunic and woven leather leggings—bore some symbol I did not recognize woven through with what appeared to be thread-of-gold. Have to admit, I coveted the boots on his feet, but I raised my eyebrow at the sheathed steel at his hip. Proof he was fake? Possibly. Possibly not. There was some debate on the issue of iron and the fae.

Other than the symbol, which I quickly sketched upon the parchment stretched across my knees, I committed his features to memory, not skilled enough with my borrowed quill to waste time and effort on secondary details. As the sharpened tip scratched across the surface, the warrior glared at me with silver-gilt eyes from beneath ebon locks that would have had any number of runway divas wanting to pull it out of jealousy. The delicate, curved point of an ear poked through as well. Either this guy was the real deal, or he was a nutjob with theatrical training. Neither possibility was quite comfortable, but I'd endured worse when on a story.

I pushed strands of ordinary brown hair out of the way behind my own ear to better see by the light of the beeswax candle held in place on the bench between us by its own drippings. Surprisingly, no fragrance rose from it. And another peculiar thing... other than the bit I'd melted to keep the whole thing standing upright, the taper hadn't burned down. The flame remained steady and bright in the surrounding darkness.

The elf cleared his throat, his impatience somehow sounding elegant, dignified. It was startling as the night was unnaturally silent, with not a trill from the night birds or chirp from a cricket. The look in his eye had grown no less intent but had taken on a puzzled air. He almost looked put out. "But *why* are you here?"

Here was a defunct bus stop at a country crossroad.

"I want to know the truth," I answered.

"The truth is a stone-cold bitch."

Wow. How raw... and crude. So at odds with the outward image; I was leaning a bit more toward him being a nutjob, but I had to be sure.

"Let's start small," I said. "The candle, why doesn't it burn down?"

"We are in Midnight."

My eyes darted to my wrist, seeking a watch that was not there. I'd been sitting here too long for it to still be midnight. "I don't understand..."

"Not midnight... *Midnight*," he answered, as if I were slow. "Some things are immutable; when you enter a crossroads at the precise moment of midnight you overlap the realm of Midnight, a place where there is no time... no boundary, only expectation. Everywhere at once and nowhere at all."

I laughed. Okay, suspicion confirmed. Nutjob.

I had a feeling I was wasting my time. I should have known by now that the truth we look for isn't always the one we find. A childhood memory had led me to this place. It was old, thin, and faded, but cherished. To be expected. I was only three years old when it happened. My family had gone camping and I'd wandered off. I was lost, alone, and frightened. It was the middle of the night at a crossroad that felt very much the same as where I found myself now. I'd cried for the knight from my picture book to save me and he had come. The next morning I'd woken up safe beside my mother with the memory already fading. Like one of my faerie tales, only I'd been so sure it was real. I *needed* to know if it was real. Gee... which one of us was delusional again?

Not wanting to think about that too hard, I fired off a question of my own: "Why are *you* here?"

This time he laughed. Rich and bold and, again, somehow familiar.

"Me?" he asked. "*I* pissed off a witch."

He laughed again and I huffed out a sigh, tired of cryptic and tired of feeling like the only one who didn't get the joke. Leaving the candle where it was and setting aside the parchment and quill, I started to reach down for my bag, halting with a shiver at a change in the air. I looked up, confused, only to be thrust to the ground. The scrape of drawn steel made my gut clench and sent me rolling beneath the weathered bench before the thought was complete. I waited for the sound of steel biting wood, or worse, flesh.

It did not come.

I peered up through the slats expecting to meet his crazed molten-silver gaze. What I saw was Elvin Warrior Dude faced off with some gawky SCA escapee. Pot-metal against Toledo steel. It was like something out of a movie; the formal challenge, the flourished salute, the nearly choreographed engagement. Well, half of the exchange anyway. Sir Gawkwin moved more like a trained bear... plenty of enthusiasm... not much grace. Slash. Jab. Clanging metal. Ringing steel. Grunts and sweat and sparks flew out from the center of the crossroad. The air carried the sharp aroma of blood.

I flinched but could not look away—though with the evidence at eye-level, part of my thoughts absently took note that still my candle did not drip, did not burn down. And then beyond all belief shining steel was struck from elvin hand and pot-metal point came to rest upon the tabard where it met smooth, pearly skin. At the tip welled a perfect ruby drop.

"Yield!" the kid half-squeaked and half-growled.

My mouth fell open as the elf went to his knees, head bowed.

I wanted to yell, to scream, to take up the sword sticking in the ground not two feet away and kick the pimply geek's ass. (Remember... delusional.) But I could only watch with fascination as the kid's expression transformed and boy became man. The cheap blade was lowered, and a more subdued salute sketched, then the guy walked away, bloodied, but unbowed.

Tension pounded a tempo against my skull. Snippets of recalled research came to mind... Hectate, Legba, vampires and ghosts and faeries... but I could scarcely reconcile them with what I'd witnessed. I closed my eyes and sought a moment of reason in the aftermath of chaos. I so wanted to believe what had transpired was a hoax, but I could not.

A weight settled on the bench while I was failing to find my zen. He made no sound, but for lightly labored breathing, which quickly steadied. I opened my eyes and glanced at him through the slats, finding myself closer to a bloodied gaping thigh than I cared to be.

"What... the hell... was that?" I managed, my voice coming out thin and my breath smelling faintly of panic.

"What he expected," was the weary answer.

I crept out from my shelter and put a bit of distance between us. Should have paid attention; I ended up between him and his sword. A good thing? A bad thing? It could go either way.

Elvin Warrior Dude sighed. Shook his head. Gave me a look that said, 'come on already.' Then he ran his hands across the rents in his clothing and over his angry wounds. I gasped and my eyes went wide. If the scent of blood weren't still in my nose, I would have wondered was I going mad. His hands began to glow, and as they passed over the damage it faded swiftly away.

"I am, and have ever been," he said, "the guardian of the four-armed crossroads. In my prideful and foolish youth, I forgot that honor bore responsibility. Hectate has seen fit to remind me. The mortal world has been seeded with legends that I must oblige."

I must have still looked confused.

"You came here seeking truth?" It was a question, but not. I nodded anyway. "That boy came desiring to prove himself in a faerie challenge."

"This is your truth: I am perceived as all things as needed... To those who believe and enter the crossroads I must be whatever they seek." Again, I thought of my research, and trembled.

"Hardly anyone comes looking for a hero," he said as if my thoughts were open to him.

And before my eyes the elvin warrior shimmered. For only a moment I caught a glimpse of the shining knight of my childhood before he sketched a salute and faded gently away.

Somewhere a cricket chirped. Only then did the scent of melting beeswax finally waft on the air.

# Mise En Place

IN THE PRE-DAWN CHILL, ERSKINE LEVO STOOD IN HER HARD-WON chef's jacket at the railing of the outdoor dining balcony, waiting for the sun to catch up with her. She had been awake for hours, making sure that all was in order for today's menu. In her kitchen, iced tubs of fresh black cod and assorted shellfish waited for her sous chef's arrival, having just been delivered direct from the docks down-city. She had already gone to the market to select the day's vegetables and herbs herself, always there first for the choicest pick. And, in an hour, the butcher would be at the door, presenting prime cuts of the other assorted proteins the elite of Kashedel would sample that evening.

But that was the evening. Right now, Erskine watched as delicate hues began to tint the lightening sky. This was her time. This cusp of potential that heralded the day. This was when she reminded herself of what she worked so hard for. Her hand slid into her pocket, poised and ready, but drew nothing out until the orb of the sun breached the horizon, shining full upon her in glorious benediction.

Basking in the glow of those first rays, Erskine turned and faced *her* restaurant, the white stucco walls rosy in the dawn light, the alternating pots of olive and lemon trees along the railings lush and vibrant, and the gold-veined marble tiles beneath the vine-draped pergola just waiting for the individual seating to be moved into place. And above it all, a neat, comfortable apartment with all the amenities she'd ever wanted and never had, eager to greet her each night.

With the evidence of her success before her, she drew the creased photograph from her pocket and allowed herself a glimpse of her family. Here, in this quiet time, the only moment of solitude she would have that day. Every day. She looked on the faces of her mother, father, and sister as she cracked the door of her heart, slowly letting out the hurt, as she would with any pressure vessel. Her family, who shunned her... who held no faith in her and turned their backs on her for wanting something different from life in a florist's shop. Wanting something more than dirt beneath her fingernails and thorns in her thumbs. Her family, who broke her heart and strengthened her resolve. Every day. A single tear slid gracefully down Erskine's cheek as she shoved the photograph in her pocket and trained her eyes on the glory that was *Erskine* the restaurant, pinnacle of Kashedel in location, refinement, and prestige.

This was her love. Her passion. Her home. The epitome of who she was.

And she took every satisfaction that her family could never afford to cross its threshold.

Erskine drew a deep breath of the morning air, scented with lemon and grape and the salt of the sea. She slowly let that breath out and drew one more deep into her belly. Her nose twitched, and she sniffed a few times, briefly wondering at the faint whiff of smoke on the breeze, before straightening her jacket and striding toward the basket and the picking knife she'd left by the glass-paned double doors. With quick, efficient motions, she culled the grapevines overhead, neatening the canopy and selecting a dozen ripe clusters for use on the day's charcuterie boards. Making her way toward the kitchen, her eyes scanned the dimly lit dining room, looking for anything out of place. She saw nothing. Her lips tipped up in satisfaction only to dip again on hearing chatter in the kitchen.

"... heard they've made their way up the coast."

"Sanja says..."

Erskine cleared her throat and pushed through the swinging doors. "mise en place," she said pointedly as she handed the basket off to her sous chef, Michi. He almost fumbled it.

"Yes, chef!"

"What does that mean, Michi?"

"Everything in its place, Chef!"

"Well... go on then!"

"Yes, chef!"

She couldn't tell if the worry in his gaze was because of his conversation, or because she'd caught him gossiping with the baker's daughter instead of starting the day's prep. Frankly, she didn't care. Turning to O'Dell, Erskine gave the girl a brusque nod, followed by a pointed look toward the back door.

As it closed behind her, the kitchen fell silent save for the sound of knives chopping.

The butcher was late, as were half her kitchen staff and all of the servers. Each time someone did arrive, fresh whiffs of smoke accompanied them, stronger and stronger as time passed.

Erskine looked up from preparing the dashi for her signature dish and frowned. "What is going on out there?"

Michi remained silent, avoiding her gaze, but his grip tightened on his knife.

Ammie, one of the servers who had just arrived, came forward, her face pale and her hands tormenting the strings of her apron. "There are fires burning below. Mother says it's just bad luck and old buildings, but I heard on the way here that General Razzin-Dahr and his men have entered the city."

Turning down the flame on the dashi, Erskine headed out to the balcony once more, wiping her hands on her apron as she went. Through the ringing in her ears, she heard the kitchen staff scrambling to follow. Michi kept pace with her, just at her back, the others strung out behind him like crumbs swept from the table. Normally, she would order all of them back to their stations, but right now her only focus was getting to the railing. Her hands gripped the marble balustrade as she looked out over the terraced cliffs of the city. She grimaced as her gaze automatically traveled to where her family's home lay, but she could not quell her relief. The houses there were undisturbed, though a smoky haze hung heavy over the neighborhood adjacent to the docks, with tendrils spreading over the city on the breeze. There were no other signs of disturbance that she could see.

While there had been talk of dissension in nearby regions and movement of military forces from distant lands, that was hardly anything new. She didn't put any store by it. People loved to speculate, especially the more common folk... and she should know. She'd grown up as common as could be. Nothing had ever come of any of the gossip the women told over the market aisles or the men shared on their front stoops. Not then, and not now.

Enough foolishness; she had meal service to prepare and a reputation for excellence to uphold.

As she entered the kitchen, her eye went toward the access staircase leading to the roof. The smoke particles filling the air outside could cause them power issues.

"Tomias... Keth... go up to the rooftop and make sure that the solar panels are clear of ash, then prep the balcony for service," Erskine ordered the idle busboys. "The rest of you... back to work! Hearsay will not shut down this kitchen today."

Choruses of "Yes, chef!" followed in her wake as she returned to her cooking.

The butcher never did arrive. Neither did any of the night's reservations or even casual diners. Erskine threw down the towel she used to clean her cook surface in disgust and glowered around the kitchen. Such waste!

"No point in standing here all night," she told her staff. "Wrap and store everything that will keep for tomorrow. Toss the rest on the compost heap."

Michi frowned and opened his mouth as if he would speak but closed it, the others just muttered 'yes, chef,' and all proceeded to do her bidding. She turned to her sous chef. Sometimes she forgot they were contemporaries, but now he watched her with a man's judgment, and she bristled.

"You wish to say something?"

His lips pressed together, and his eyes darkened as if he debated with himself on the wisdom of speaking. Then he straightened ever so slightly beneath her gaze and gave a nod.

"Yes, chef... please, might the leavings go to the soup kitchen? I would be glad to take them—"

"As your day's wages?" she interrupted him. He grimaced at that, disappointment in his gaze as he shook his head. She felt a hint of shame kindled by his expression. She quickly smothered it, then went on the offensive. "I paid good money for these provisions. If I do not recoup that cost one way," she said, gesturing toward the empty dining room, "I must another. The leavings will go on the compost heap. At least then I will gain value from the food we grow from it. Understood?"

He looked as if he would say more, but only nodded before turning away to wrap and stow the materials on his station, his shoulders lifting in a silent sigh. She thought that was the end of it, but he took a deeper breath and straightened once more before turning back to her.

"There is value in showing goodwill to those around you. In helping those in need."

He then turned back to his task without waiting for her to respond. Erskine frowned deeper, vexed that his opinion should matter to her. She had believed as he did once... until her mentor, Savan, nearly ended her career over such an act of kindness.

Erskine was about to send the staff home early when the bell on the front door sounded. All eyes snapped to the swinging doors, but no one moved. Moments later, the hostess, Aliz, entered the kitchen.

"Your... your presence is requested on the balcony, chef," she said, her expression neutral, but her gaze panicked.

Before any of the others could move, Erskine silently motioned them to stay back, including Aliz. She then stripped off her spattered apron and smoothed her hair before pushing through the swinging doors. With dignity, she wended her way past too many empty tables as she headed for the balcony, seething inside at the waste of her time and resources. While she hated to give credence to rumors...

Erskine's steps faltered for a heartbeat as she passed through the glass-paned doors.

She hated it even worse when rumors were true.

Seated just beneath the pergola, with a clear view of the city, was a host of men in military garb. Hanging braziers took the chill off the night as they lit the four hastily combined tables, glinting off the cutlery as well as a dizzying variety of medals and satin campaign ribbons, all of them meaningless to Erskine. The man most decorated bore signs of Truktanese ancestry—a square jaw, painfully high cheekbones, and narrow eyes—to go with his hairless head.

Razzin-Dahr stood as Erskine approached and greeted her with arms spread. "Ah! The acclaimed Chef Levo, at last!"

Gratifying as that might have been from anyone else, Erskine knew not to trust such an informal greeting from this infamous man. If she were to believe his reputation, there were layers to his intentions, and they often lacked in veracity. Erskine halted just out of reach and, with her arms straight at her sides, accorded him a brief but respectful bow.

"Gentlemen, how may I serve you tonight?" she asked, cordially acknowledging the General's dozen or so subordinates, while she thought on what could be made quickly and in sufficient quantity with the ingredients left in the larder. "May I recommend our charcuterie board and fresh bread, followed by the Dashi with Miso Black Cod and Greens, paired with our house blend matcha-and-ginger infused white wine, and a clarified lemon soufflé with honey gastrique to finish?"

Most of the men looked at her with blank gazes, clearly not having the faintest knowledge of fine dining. Razzin-Dahr looked only slightly less lost but covered it well with a faint moue.

"No bourbon custard with oatmeal tuile and candied basil?" he asked.

Her eyes widened, and she nearly clutched the chair back in front of her. That was her dish, but not one she had ever served at *Erskine*. Very few were familiar with it... all of them far away in Allendis, where she'd perfected the recipe. Hiding her discomfort behind a demure smile, she pressed her hands together and briefly inclined her head. "I am afraid not. I can offer a rice-flour chocolate torte with rose-petal-and-pistachio brittle if the soufflé does not suit."

In the guise of waiting for his reply, she closely examined the General. She knew *of* him—his face, his exploits, the darker rumors—who didn't? But she had never served him that she was aware. Of course, in the years she traveled the many lands of Pangaea learning her craft the hard way, she had never enjoyed such status as she did today. This man should not know enough to connect her with a dish another had taken credit for. No matter, though. However he knew, he knew, and that made her rather uncomfortable. Razzin-Dahr had sought out her restaurant for a purpose, and it wasn't merely to share a meal with his men.

Suppressing a shudder, she could stand there no more. "Gentlemen, if you will excuse me, I shall return to the kitchen to prepare your first course while you decide. Please inform Aliz as to your choice of dessert." As she turned to leave, she noticed fresh plumes of smoke darkening the twilight over the city and could not help but gasp softly.

She would never forget the smug look on Razzin-Dahr's face as he heard her.

The General and his men stayed long into the night, eating the recommended menu and much of the stores she had counted on for the next day. They stayed long enough that Erskine ordered the remaining staff home. All but Michi and Aliz complied. The three of them moved around the inside dining room like ghosts, nominally shutting down the front end for the night, though there was little actually to be done.

As they finished, Erskine felt the nerves along her back twitch. She knew the men watched. What she didn't know was why they lingered. Other than eating like a ravenous horde, they had offered no offense, save their laughter and cheers as they looked down on the burning city below. While she had to admit *Erskine* had the best view to be had, she doubted that was what had brought them here.

Enough, however, was enough. Shooing the others into the kitchen, Erskine headed for the balcony only to find Razzin-Dahr standing in the doorway.

She maintained a professional demeanor and did not flinch away.

"How else can we help you?" she asked.

"I have chosen you for my new personal chef."

At that, she jerked.

"Excuse me? I am flattered, but I have a restaurant to tend to already."

He looked around with a smirk and gestured at the empty dining room. "Do you? A building, perhaps, and a very nice one, but you seem to find yourself a bit lacking in clientele, no? And goodness, have you seen?" He took her arm and drew her forward as he moved to the railing. "Even buildings don't last forever. Just look. All those people losing their livelihoods... losing their dreams..."

The implied threat in his comment did not go unnoticed.

Erskine tensed and felt her gorge rise as she looked out over the city she loved. Flames stood out bright against the moonless night. Not one neighborhood was free of them. She could not imagine how the whole city did not burn at this point. How many of those buildings belonged to people she knew?

"And where would I cook, as your personal chef?"

"I have brought the commissary caravan my former chef used."

At that she did recoil. "I think not!" she told him, not caring in that instance how he would react. Righteous indignation dripped from her words. "Here we stand in a premier, fully appointed restaurant, and you would have me cook out of a rolling chow hall? I could not fit a quarter of my equipment or any of my staff in one of those cooking closets. We will not even discuss provisions..."

As soon as she was finished, Erskine regretted her tone, if not her words.

The General, however, had the grace to laugh. Boisterously.

"This is a rather nice place if a bit much for just my officers and me. It will serve when I don't require you to be elsewhere."

Erskine wisely remained silent, though her brow creased at his comment.

"If that will be all," she said to the group in general. "We must close for the night."

And still, the men made no move to leave.

Her muscles tensing with each moment that passed, Erskine softly cleared her throat and turned to leave the balcony, calling back over her shoulder, "If you gentlemen would be so kind? I must ask that you leave. We rise early to prep for the evening's clientele."

Razzin-Dahr appeared in front of her before she took two steps. The back of his hand struck her cheek hard, sending her to the ground. She cried out as her head cracked against the marble tile. Her mouth filled with the copper-penny taste of blood and her ears with the muffled laughter of the General's men. Before she could focus or react, a shadow dropped down from the pergola above. Erskine looked up, her vision swimming.

Michi crouched over her, legs braced and muscles taut like he planned to take on the whole host. He must have been spying from the rooftop. Before he did something foolish, Erskine reached up to grab his arm, using the leverage to haul herself to her feet. He shifted to better support her. Once she gained her footing—and her composure—she looked up.

Razzin-Dahr sneered at the both of them, but his eyes locked with hers.

"You no longer give the orders here. Understood?" he said, his tone cold and his gaze smoldering. "No one gives orders in Kashedel except for me."

Trembling, Erskine lowered her gaze and nodded, teeth clenched against the heated words trying to force themselves out.

Apparently satisfied, the General motioned his men to the door.

"Oh, and Chef Levo," he called out, looking back over his shoulder. "I said, *personal* chef. There will be no other clientele."

Michi showed up in the morning, but no one else.

Erskine hadn't even been to the market. She sat at the staff break table in the corner of the kitchen, glowering into space. He came over to her. With a gentle touch, he lifted her chin, checked her bruised cheek and peered close into her eyes.

"Any double vision?" he asked. "Headache?"

She grimaced and jerked her head back, wincing as the dull ache she'd had since she woke up spiked. Michi frowned, and Erskine watched as he went to the tea chest. Soon the aromas of willow bark and chamomile filled the kitchen, followed by the sharp, clean scents of lemon and honey as he placed a mug of tea in front of her.

"Drink."

Erskine didn't argue. She wrapped her chilled hands around the warm ceramic mug and brought it to her lips, breathing in the fragrant steam and willing it to soothe her. Not that it stood a chance. Michi sat down across from her. She could tell by his expression he had more news to share. News she likely wouldn't want to hear.

"Go on..." she told him quietly.

He drew a deep breath and ran a hand over his face. Before he could speak, the back door opened without warning. In the alley stood an eyesore of a caravan. Presumably, the rolling chow hall. The General's men steadily unloaded it, filing into the kitchen, each of them carrying a carton or two. Erskine started to push to her feet, mouth open to demand an explanation when Michi placed a hand on her shoulder and gently pushed her back down with a subtle shake of his head. The men set their burdens on the counter and then filed back out in a steady stream. All in silence. She didn't recognize any of them.

Within ten minutes, the men were gone and Erskine's kitchen was fully provisioned, though she had no idea with what. The caravan still sat in her alley like a looming threat.

Erskine turned to look at Michi.

He sighed deeply and then met her gaze. "The butcher shop has burned to the ground. It is said, but not very loudly, that Mitron refused to comply when Razzin-Dahr claimed the contents of his shop to feed his forces. That is but one of the stories being told, but they are pretty much all the same."

Erskine swallowed hard and looked around her kitchen before settling her gaze back on Michi. Her imagination painted everything in flames.

She shuddered uncontrollably and squeezed her eyes closed tight only to snap them open again, realizing the visions in her head were worse.

Other than the air of tension that permeated the restaurant—indeed, all of Kashedel—life mostly went back to normal. Michi showed up faithfully each day, and about a third of the staff returned as well. Erskine cooked. And cooked. And cooked. Though her clientele was more elite than previously, and never paid, provisions were provided, and she and her staff were safe. Their situation felt precarious, but when hadn't it? Even before the takeover, Erskine had always been aware her fortunes could change. That was why she worked so hard. Nothing had changed there, save she worked for their safety. While she could, she paid the staff; even when she couldn't, she fed them. Life went on. It always did.

Until it didn't.

Though daily provisions magically paraded through the kitchen door—more than they could possibly need even for a full house—Erskine was given no say in what arrived. Most days, she could manage with whatever was there. Today she received orders to serve her specialty, the Dashi with Miso Black Cod and Greens. With only half the ingredients delivered.

She would have to go to the market and pray fortune provided. Rather than send one of the staff, Erskine went herself, needing a moment's respite from the kitchen, her haven-turned-prison. She gathered what coin she had, along with a few easily carried delicacies to use for barter and retrieved her shawl from behind the door before calling out to Michi.

"Continue the prep. I won't be long."

He looked up from the daikon he was dicing, concern in his gaze, but he just nodded and murmured, "Yes, chef."

Erskine wrapped her shawl around her shoulders and draped it like a hood over her head before descending into the city. It was the first time she'd left the restaurant, or her small apartment above it, since the occupation. She had received word that her family was safe, and presumed life went unchanged for the majority of the city's occupants.

She had presumed wrong.

Rather than heading right for the market, she wandered down the terraces and through the neighborhoods, seeing for herself the drastic changes in her home. Tension had settled into each crack and crevice of the city. There were soldiers everywhere, wandering the streets as if on a stroll, or positioned strategically on duty. They didn't belong here. Pretending to be a part of life as if they had always been, just like the palpable fear seasoning the air. Locals no longer lingered to chat in the streets. They hurried from point to point, eyes down and shoulders hunched. She saw more sunken cheeks than ever before, and the gazes she managed to meet were fearful, angry, or vacant and glassy-eyed.

Though the fires no longer burned, there were plenty of piles of charred timbers. Enough that the smoky scent of fire superseded the usual salty tang of the sea. That alone made it seem Erskine walked someplace other than her home, but combined with the hush that blanketed the city, it made her feel as if she wandered a spectral land.

Without any intent, Erskine found herself standing before her parent's florist shop. She gasped and nearly crumbled beneath the unexpected blow as she looked up in disbelief. A brand-new sign hung above the picture window where bouquets of flowers once stood, fragrant and cheerful. In their place were piles of foreign goods. Tobacco and liquor and luxury items quite out of place in the depressed atmosphere Erskine had traveled through to get here. Even the faces behind the counter were unknown to her.

She was loathe to go in, but she knew no one else to ask of the fate of her family. All that was familiar was gone. Approaching the counter, she suppressed a spurt of anger. The shopkeeper was wearing a garment Erskine recognized as her mother's. The woman looked her up and down before sniffing in distaste.

"How may I help you?" she said with a practiced smile.

"Please... could you tell me where I can find the florist?" Erskine asked.

The smile vanished, and a subtle sneer lifted one side of the woman's lip. "Either buy something or go away, I do not have time to waste on idle chitchat." Erskine let her gaze trail from the dust rag in the woman's hand to the empty shop before lifting one brow. She then pivoted and, with the dignity of a premier chef, left the shop, letting the door slam behind her.

She headed directly for her parents' house but saw no sign of life. The doors were locked, and no one came to her knocking. At her childhood home or the surrounding houses. But then, she'd likely frightened anyone lurking behind those closed doors with her pounding and shouts.

As she turned and walked away, righteous rage blossomed in her heart, fed on much kindling as she continued to see for herself the harm her beloved Kashedel had taken at the calloused hands of Razzin-Dahr. Her hand slid into the pocket of her chef's jacket, unconsciously smoothing the crinkled edges of her family's photograph. She tried not to imagine the worst, but the state of the city made that difficult.

Kashedel had not only lost its life, but also its soul.

Nowhere was this more evident than the marketplace. When she saw the state it was in, Erskine gasped at the transformation. No friendly barter. No haggling or strategic examination of the goods. What merchants there were had sparse stock to offer, even for that hour of the day, and much of it lacking in the quality that had been available just last month.

It was too much. The city. Her family. Her restaurant. Battered and abused until the spirit had gone out of them. While the evil slug responsible dined in luxury, the people starved. He wasted more food in one night than many of the people had in a week, since the occupation. Upon that realization, Erskine's thoughts stumbled on a rope of guilt. True, she had not stolen from the people or oppressed them, but she had certainly lived a privileged life of late, with no care for those forced to choose daily between food and necessities. She tossed perfectly good scraps and kitchen waste on the compost each night. No more. That would change going forward. She would find her family and feed her people.

Trembling with tension and anger, she made her way to her usual stalls and gathered all of the missing ingredients but one. The black cod. She stood before the fishmonger's stall staring at the meager piles of fish. Not a cod of any color among them. In the past, she had substituted whitefish with little difference in the final results, but for some reason, she lingered, undecided, her fingers running over a pile of bubble fish—a delicacy she did not often serve given the inherent risk. While the flesh titillated the tongue, if improperly prepared it would stop the heart and other vital organs. Or, if the diner were very lucky, merely plague them with stomach and bowel distress, followed by several days of paralysis. Erskine knew how to prepare it properly, but chose not to take the chance. She preferred not to gamble the reputation of her restaurant unnecessarily. And still, her fingers ran over the iced fish.

An uneducated palate would scarcely notice, were bubble fish substituted for black cod.

Even taking a lift trolley, Erskine was late returning to the restaurant. She scrambled off the back without waiting for the stop, already stripping off her shawl as she entered the kitchen, relieved to see her parcels arrived before her. Michi met her at the door with a fresh chef's jacket. She started to wave it away when she noticed the grey tinge of ash across her sleeve. With her back to the rest of the staff, she quickly shucked the soiled jacket and accepted the fresh. Before she had it fully buttoned, the swinging doors swished behind her.

Erskine carefully schooled her expression before turning around. Taking the time to secure her jacket, she pivoted with her spine straight and her shoulders back. Aliz stood by the doors, impeccably put together, but frazzled and under strain to those who knew the signs to look for.

"Yes?" Erskine asked.

"Your presence is requested on the balcony."

"Thank you, Aliz. I will be right out."

Erskine then turned to Michi. "Prep out the whitefish, leave the rest."

He nodded, but when she started to move off, he reached out and caught her arm. When she whipped around, he let go but nodded at her face and hands. "You'll want to clean up first."

Erskine blushed, then nodded. "Thank you."

In the past, her confidence had been a part of her uniform. Today, it was a part of her armor. She made her way to the balcony as if she still ruled her small domain, studiously looking past the signs of abuse that marred the once-sparkling finish on the culinary jewel of Kashedel.

The General sat in audience beneath the burning braziers with his usual entourage of officers and ass-kissers surrounding him. Sprinkled among them were members of the city's elite and a woman or two huddled beside the more senior officers, including Razzin-Dahr himself. In general, Erskine did her best not to take note of these poor unfortunates. Not once had they ever appeared willing. They were ornamental, not even allowed to eat the food she prepared. Tonight, however, one of them caught her eye. Erskine nearly stopped dead, her gaze locking on that familiar face. Reflexively, her hand went to the pocket of her chef's jacket only to find it empty, her photograph in the jacket recently removed. It had been years since she'd seen her sister in person, but she knew that face, beneath its brash makeup and poorly hidden bruises.

"Malikay," she whispered, no more than a breath, too low for anyone to hear, let alone her sister. She then drew herself up and moved forward as if nothing were out of order. She should have had a career on the stage. Within, Erskine's blood boiled as she catalogued each mark marring her sister's skin and wondered at those she could not see. Tamping those feelings down, she halted beside the General and accorded him the briefest of bows.

Apparently, Michi had been covering for her. Before Razzin-Dahr sat a rather well-executed rendition of her recipe for shrimp and sausage crumble over red-pepper polenta, a popular starter at *Erskine*. She had known for some time Michi was wasted as a sous chef. Here was proof. The dish, however, had been picked over, barely sampled.

"This is subpar," the General grumbled, his broad brow hanging low in a scowl. "I expect more from my personal chef. Take it away and get your act together. This kitchen is a disgrace." He backhanded the dish, sending it flying. It slammed into Erskine's chest and spattered her face with the contents. Malikay gasped, but Erskine did not react. Pressing her lips closed tight—tasting bitter rage and well-seasoned polenta—she pivoted and returned to the kitchen.

And still, she said nothing.

Going to her workstation, she found everything set out precisely as she preferred it, spices measured to her left, vegetables to the right, raw proteins iced before her.

"*mise en place...*" she murmured. "Everything in its place..." Only not everything was, beyond this kitchen.

She ran her fingers over the whitefish. There were many people outside. Perhaps more than she could serve with just this... Abruptly, she turned, pinning Michi with a gaze.

"Why don't they fight? Why doesn't anyone resist?"

"You saw today, didn't you? Too many soldiers, too many weapons. A tyrant that will take everything but their lives just to see them suffer for their impudence. Some plan, but none are brave enough to act without the perfect opportunity, not when it might mean more suffering for their loved ones."

She had seen. Perhaps for the first time with eyes opened wide.

Erskine nodded and reached for the bubble fish. With quick, efficient motions, she cleaned and filleted each one until it was almost impossible to tell bubble from whitefish. Whenever she encountered roe, she scooped the choicest pearls and slid them into her dashi pot, letting the flavor enhance the broth. The roe was where the danger was, along with the liver and other such organs. Cooking did not kill the toxin, but the broth would dilute it, She was a chef, after all, not a murderer. Providence willing, however, and Razzin-Dahr and his men would know pain before paralysis took them. Whatever happened after that—once Michi returned with those poised to resist the General—could only best be described as justice.

Michi said nothing as she plated up the dishes, garnishing the one meant for Razzin-Dahr with three flawless pearls of roe. She turned to her sous chef when she was done.

"Perfect... don't you think?" Erskine asked him with a pointed look.

"Impossible to resist."

Then, with a satisfied smile and understanding in his gaze, he headed out the back door, clearly on a mission.

Erskine motioned the servers forward and oversaw while they balanced multiple bowls along their arms as trained, not one of them spilling a drop or disturbing the careful arrangement of each dish. As they headed for the swinging doors, she picked up the General's entrée herself and followed them out to the balcony.

Erskine held her sister's gaze as she approached the table and let the memories of all the devastation she had seen that day play across her thoughts. She felt no guilt as she placed the dish before Razzin-Dahr. In the kitchen and in life, it was important for everything to be in its place.

This was not his place.

# Mama Bear

A Tale of the Wild Hunt

Something wasn't right. Except lately, a lot wasn't right. Made it hard to tell if this was something new or just the same ol' stuff picking at her nerves. Suzanne Cosain, fae exile and founding member of the Wild Hunt MC, downshifted and let up on the throttle as she approached the intersection. Her half-human husband, Lance, slowed to a stop next to her. She heard his whiskey-rich voice murmur from her helmet speaker.

"You doin' okay, babe?"

She nodded as she opened up the throttle again, though she expected it was a lie. A white one, but still a lie. He didn't push her as he took position to her right and just behind her, letting her take Front Door. Good thing, because she hadn't a clue what to say. She felt wired. Poised for a fight. Half the time protective—though she had no clue of what—the other half twenty kinds of pissed off. One moment jubilant, the next melancholy. Life had become one constant emotional barrage. Her skin felt too tight, and her nerves buzzed with energy. Every smell was amped up, and nothing tasted right. Was it her curse, or had something else come along to screw with her? Still, the sun felt amazing, and the wind in her face cleared the fog she'd woken up in. Swerving around a road gator—remnants left by some trucker's blow-out— she gunned it and took off down the empty stretch of road, her silver-blond hair whipping around her bare shoulders and leather halter top.

Lance's laughter filled her headspace, lightening her mood. He drew up next to her, then pushed to pass. "You're on," he crowed, speaking into his mic a bit louder to be heard over the engines as he revved his Knucklehead. More than ready to play, Suzanne opened the throttle on her Harley Softail even further.

As they raced down the back country road, Lance's thick, segmented ponytail lashing behind him, Suzanne suddenly sensed mischief of a fae sort. She didn't slow down, but she did let her otherworldly sense play out, scanning the area around them.

She laughed abruptly.

"Looks like your *friend* is looking to get back a bit of his own," she said into her mic as she brought all her attention back to the road. The ride had begun to get rougher: Wrinkles in the asphalt, an increase in potholes, a network of cracks like you'd find in the deep desert. She wasn't worried. She and Lance both had ride bells hanging off their bikes, spelled with protections against road gremlins.

Lance growled in annoyance, and Suzanne felt the build-up as he drew power until his shoulder fins unfurled through the slits in his jacket and tendrils of energy arched from his back. She heard him call out with his thoughts as he let his iridescent white "wings" flare.

"Cut it out, Smear," he growled, addressing the embodiment of the Road. *Every* road. The little bugger held something of a grudge against The Wild Hunt, the club's leader, in particular. That would be Lance. "Not today..."

The road conditions just continued to get rougher, and the breeze carried the sound of grumbling just low enough that Suzanne couldn't make out the words. The tone carried loud and clear, though, as her front wheel jittered to the side, slipping on the edge of a tar snake she could have sworn hadn't been there a moment before. Suzanne managed to straighten the Softail out, but her patience waned.

Not finding the situation funny anymore, she also started drawing power. Her fins unfurled with a snap until energy crackled across her bare back in what she knew were lavender and blue "wings" with rosy accents that deepened to red and black when her curse got the better of her. From the snap of the current, she expected those hues were darkening. Ever since she'd taken revenge on a murder of redcaps, her nature had grown more... complicated... volatile. Or, as Lance liked to put it, bloodthirsty.

Literally.

She'd ended the redcaps who'd attacked her but in the fight had somehow claimed the leader's cap for her own. At the time, she hadn't known the nature of the beastie. The creature she slew wasn't the redcap, the "hat" was. A parasitic fae that corrupted the nature of whatever host it glommed on to. Or tried to, anyway. She'd come under a constant barrage of emotional assault ever since, sly and subtle one moment, hitting her like a sledgehammer the next. Suzanne was giving it the fight of her life until she found a way to break free. Just... sometimes, she lost ground. Emotions were Lance's strength. He'd spent most of his life as an empath, with no access to his mage talent. Suzanne, on the other hand, had been emotionally repressed right up until the day she'd broken free from her father's control and fled to the mortal realm.

Even thinking about it sent a red haze over her vision.

The air grew heavy with tension, and the sunlight took on a hard edge. Pissed at how everyone seemed to think they could mess with her life, she summoned a mage bolt.

"Back it down, Sue," Lance murmured, both his tone and his link to her reaching out to sooth her agitation. "He's just trying to get us riled. Things are already smoothing out."

Fighting the urge to lash out anyway, Suzanne nodded, slowly releasing her grip on the energy and letting it flow back into the natural channels she'd drawn it from. She looked over at Lance as they continued to ride like nothing had happened. It was hardly a surprise when he took the lead. Neither was the direction they headed. The road they were on led straight to *Delilah's*, the bar they—and the Wild Hunt MC—called home.

When they rode up, the front lot was empty. Not unexpected. It was the middle of the day on a Wednesday. Suzanne pulled up right next to the entrance, just off to the side, and shut the bike down, backing slightly to set the center stand. Lance pulled in next to her and left his Knucklehead idling.

"I'm headin' over to my dad's; the camshaft's sticking."

Suzanne hesitated, feeling a sense of unease. "No problem. You want me to have Mongo fix you something, or wait until you get back?"

"Nah, I'll grab something at Cam's," Lance said as he backed the bike up. "I'll probably spend a little time with him. It's been a while now that the Knucklehead's running again."

That sense of unease came back. Lance's bike had been totaled not that long ago… the *first* time he encountered Smear face-to-face. Suzanne's gaze ran over him, making sure he wore his leathers, his helmet framing the strong angles of his face. Her urge to protect him welled up even stronger than before. An image formed in her mind of Lance's body broken and the light gone out of his warm brown eyes. Beneath her breath, she growled. While she wasn't above worrying about those that mattered to her, the image had the distinct feel of the redcap's influence.

Suzanne slammed the door on those thoughts as she caught her lip curling in a snarl. She hid it by lifting off her helmet and setting it on her engine before swinging her leg over the back to stand between the bikes.

"Hey… you all right?" Lance asked, reaching out to kill his engine.

Suzanne gritted her teeth and forced herself to calm. She and Lance had a connection… a literal connection, even before they'd wed. Lance felt whatever she felt unless she took an effort to block it. Something she vowed to him never to do again.

She leaned over his bike to stop him.

"No. I'm fine, just a little out of sorts. Go on and get that checked out. Can't have you eating asphalt again."

Lance nodded, then stole a kiss before turning back to the road. Something in Suzanne's gut twisted uncomfortably as she watched him ride away.

"You comin' in or what?"

Suzanne jerked around at the unexpected voice. Man, she was on edge. Delilah—as in *the* Delilah—stood in the open door, just shaking her head. Suzanne's eyes locked on the tendrils of fiery red hair bobbing around the woman's shoulders. A shudder went through her as the curse tried to take hold.

"Girl, get your ass in here. I ain't air-conditioning the outside!" Delilah's words were sharp, but her expression was worried.

It was strange. Just at the sight of Lance's aunt, the tension flowed out of Suzanne, and her heart flooded with joy. She'd never had a mother that she could remember. That didn't bother her one bit anymore. Suzanne's birth mother would never have been as strong as Delilah. Suzanne's father, Callan, wouldn't have stood for it. He would have *hated* Delilah just for being herself, let alone for being human. That just made Suzanne love the woman more.

Making sure her bike was secure, Suzanne went inside, dropping a kiss on Delilah's cheek as she passed. That earned Suzanne a strange look. As much as Delilah loved her as if she'd birthed her—and Suzanne had no doubt she did—it wasn't like casual kisses were their thing.

But then, the kiss hadn't been casual.

Suzanne couldn't explain it, but right now, her hyped-up emotions were all over the place... not just the constant aggression that simmered under the surface since she'd gotten herself stuck with the 'cap, but all of her emotions. Not knowing what to say, Suzanne just murmured, "Thanks, 'Lilah," as she headed for the kitchen.

"Hey! You leave my cook alone!" Delilah called after her.

"I'm hungry!" Suzanne yelled back.

Delilah's shocked silence was a tangible thing. It weighed so heavy on Suzanne's shoulders, she shrugged them to try and rid herself of the sensation. When she glanced back, she caught Delilah trying to hide a smile.

Suzanne didn't eat much. She didn't need to, but everyone still worried, particularly once the secret of her curse had come out. Energy had to come from somewhere. Better for her... Hell, better for *all* of them that it be a clean source.

Resisting the urge to fidget beneath Delilah's gaze, Suzanne smiled back. "I'm asking Mongo for some pasta primavera, you want some?" What she really wanted was a super-rare steak, but that was courting trouble until she found a way around the curse.

Delilah shook her head. "You go on, sweetie. I gotta take care of some clean-up in the backroom before the lunch crowd comes in. Sammy's boys have been rooting through the airgun equipment."

Suzanne had a plan...

... then she walked through the swinging kitchen doors.

The sweet, savory aroma of root-beer-braised pulled pork reached out and grabbed her by the salivary glands. Her belly rumbled, and her mouth grew juicy. She knew better, though... she didn't say a word. Skirting the prep stations and cook area, Suzanne squatted down next to Garm, Mongo's beat-up beast of a mutt, curled up quiet like by the back door. No one knew the pup's story, but he bore a hell of a lot of scars. So did Suzanne, but Garm's everyone could see. Mongo went soft whenever someone showed his dog some love. Not that Suzanne wouldn't have anyway, but as she scratched Garm's scruff, she looked over her shoulder at the cook.

"Hey, Mongo..."

"Yeah, yeah..." He cut her off. "You ain't foolin' anyone."

Suzanne smiled and gave the dog a quick squeeze before standing up and turning toward Delilah's secret weapon. Mongo was as far from a greasy-spoon fry cook as Garm was from a pedigreed bitch. He had the chops—and the credentials—to cook in any Michelin-Star restaurant. *Delilah's* suited him best.

"I'm feeling peckish," she admitted. An understatement, but such a rare confession that Mongo cocked his head at her as if maybe he hadn't heard her right. "I would love some pasta primavera..." Mongo looked highly pleased until she added, "... with a huge scoop of that pulled pork on top..." She nearly laughed at the brief flash of horror that flickered across the cook's face as his inner-chef rebelled at the very concept. Mongo just nodded, though, turning back to his cook area and prepping for her meal.

For a while, Suzanne watched. Until Mongo just barely nicked his finger as he chopped the vegetables. At the sight of the tiny drop of blood that welled up, a whole other appetite rose. Suzanne gritted her teeth and squeezed her eyes shut, fighting the wave of blood-thirst back as she headed for the swinging doors. "Sorry, Mongo..."

He called after her, but Suzanne just quickened her steps as she moved through the bar and across the backroom to the stairs leading to the second-floor apartments. Two steps at a time and she stood before her door, breathing heavy and struggling to unclench her fists. When she saw the state of her hands, she cursed like a truck driver. Blood welled up from her palms in crimson crescents where her nails had dug in.

"You're upsetting the baby."

"FUCK!" Suzanne whirled around, more than fed up with people sneaking up on her at this point. Lance's cousin Tilly stood in the door of the other apartment, the one she shared with her parents, Delilah and Jonraphal, Lance's full-fae blood uncle.

Tilly had an odd, dreamy look on her face like she wasn't even half there. Lost in some kind of trance or as if she'd reverted to the childlike, brain-damaged state she had been in just months ago, before Lance's magic had whisked away the veil trapping her in her own mind. But not quite.

"I said, you're upsetting the baby. Stop it," Tilly repeated, then she swayed, just catching herself on the door jamb.

Suzanne started forward to help her, reaching out, then she saw her bloodied hands and drew them back. What the hell was going on? When Tilly blinked and looked at her, a touch confused, Suzanne just threw up her hands and snapped, "How do you think I feel?" before turning away to open her own door, not even caring how many bloody fingerprints she left anymore.

"Don't," Tilly murmured, suddenly beside her. The girl reached into Suzanne's pocket and tugged out the plastic baggy holding the redcap. "I don't know what happened, but you need to feed it anyway."

It took all of Suzanne's effort to rein back her rage as she snatched the bloody parasite from her friend's hand. A sense of satisfaction not her own flared in the back of Suzanne's thoughts as she ran the 'cap over her bloody skin. It tried to get greedy, tried to suck its fill from the wounds, but Suzanne dug her nails in hard, along with her stubborn will. She winced at the creature's mental shriek. "Too bad, you moist fucking leech. Be happy I don't shove you into Mongo's dehydrator and be done with you."

Only she couldn't, could she... ? If the 'cap died, so did she. Hell, she couldn't even be far away from it without being crippled with pain.

But then... maybe that wouldn't be such a bad trade-off. Of course, plenty of people would argue to the death against that thought. She shoved the redcap into its zipper bag and shoved the bag back into her pocket before turning to confront Tilly.

"And while we're at it, what the hell baby are you talking about?"

Tilly just blinked and, with a slight frown, said, "Baby?"

Suzanne just shook her head and turned back to her door.

"Forget it," she said with a weary sigh, totally done with what had turned into a shit stick of a day. She didn't realize tears streamed down her face until Tilly reached out to wipe them away.

"Are you okay?"

The tears just came harder until Suzanne had to bite back a sob. All she could do was shake her head. There was no answer she could give.

"Here, dumplin', take this."

Suzanne's head snapped up, hardly believing what she heard, but there Lance stood with Tilly beside him, holding a covered plate. At the sight of it, Suzanne finally noticed an aroma so enticing, her stomach forced its way past all the negativity to be heard in one loud rolling rumble. Loud enough that she startled a laugh from Lance, but he quickly sobered.

"You were going to Cam's," she managed to get out.

Lance nodded, his lips pressing tight a moment as his gaze clouded. "Got the feeling I needed to be here," he answered as he pulled her into his arms.

"What's wrong, angel?" he asked softly as his lips pressed a gentle kiss just above her ear.

For a moment, Suzanne hugged him tight, then just as quickly, she pushed him away.

In what even she had to admit was a petulant tone, she muttered beneath her breath, "I'm hungry."

Lance laughed again.

"We could tell," he said as he reached over and took the plate back from Tilly, holding it out to Suzanne with a quirked brow. "Mongo sent this up for you, said you asked for it... special."

Suzanne drooled. Actually drooled. And she didn't give a damn either.

Nearly snatching the plate, she lifted the lid and tried to pick at the pork at the same time.

"On that note," Tilly said, her tone wry, "I'm late for my lunch shift downstairs."

Suzanne barely heard her, finally managing to get a pinch of the barbeque-laden meat past her lips. "Mmmmmmm..."

"How about we get you inside, and then you can go to town on that?" Lance said with a chuckle, his eyes filled with mingled swirls of both love and concern.

Giving him a guilty look, Suzanne couldn't even begin to explain. She just replaced the cloche and stepped back out of the way so Lance could open the door.

Her husband fed her and cared for her and then took her to bed. At some point, they even slept. As they drifted off for the last time, she remembered what Tilly had said. Pushing past a yawn, she murmured to Lance, "What baby was Tilly talking about?"

Lance just gave a soft snore.

Suzanne woke up screaming. Flat out, blood-curdling screaming. Lance jerked awake beside her and before the last scream faded, crouched over her on the bed looking for the threat, the soft white glow of his unfurling wings banishing the glistening crimson from her nightmare.

She lay there with a death grip on the sheets and the cries of a baby fading beneath her own panting breath. If only she could banish the image of a wizened, shark-toothed face staring up from her own arms.

Moving slowly, Lance dropped back down to the bed and gently pulled her into his arms, persisting until she relaxed into him. It took a while. Even once she accepted that she was safe and sheltered, her body shook in faint tremors slow to fade.

"Wanna talk about it?" he murmured by her ear.

Suzanne gave a short, sharp shake of her head.

"'Kay." And he snuggled just a bit closer. In minutes, his measured breath ruffled her hair, and his arms relaxed around her. The one across her waist slid down to her belly, and something in her gut fluttered at the touch, shifted, as if pressing up to get closer. At the sensation, dread settled over Suzanne as realization dawned.

Slowly, her hand joined Lance's, and she extended her otherworldly senses.

"Ah, shit..." she muttered through clenched teeth, every muscle suddenly tense. What was she going to do?

The nestled glow within her flinched, and Suzanne bit back another curse as Lance shifted fitfully behind her. Doubt and hurt bubbled up, and the presence shrank back more, as if uncertain of its welcome. Suzanne instantly reached out, cradling her belly and crushing her fear, letting the warmth of her love flow over the little one. Her emotions whirled out of control, bombarding her with fear and joy and disbelief, but most of all astonishment as she encountered this brand-new soul... with the crappy luck of being dependent on her. Then terror rose up, overwhelming everything else. Suzanne's belly cramped, and her stomach heaved, then she was scrambling from the bed and into the bathroom, pausing only to snatch up the hated 'cap from the nightstand, lest the straining link between them made matters worse.

She'd barely wrapped herself around the porcelain bowl when Lance came up behind her. With one hand, he held her hair out of the way. With the other, he rubbed gentle circles at the base of her back. When she'd finished heaving, he cleaned her up, took her in his arms, and carried her to bed. All while she clutched that damned little zipper bag. She wished the thing to the deepest depths infinitely more than she had before.

How could she keep a little one safe when she couldn't even save herself?

In the morning, Suzanne woke to find Lance watching her.

She suspected her smile came out more of a grimace. Her husband just leaned over and ran his lips over hers before drawing her into the shelter of his arms.

"Ready to talk?"

Breathing a sigh, Suzanne nodded and snuggled in closer, soaking in the sense of peace and security. Her mind, on the other hand, frantically scrambled with where to start. So long, in fact, Lance leaned back and peered into her face.

"With words this time?"

Suzanne laughed despite the tension in her belly.

"I dreamed... I dreamed the redcap took over our child."

Lance drew a sharp breath, and his brow dipped in confusion. Before he could speak, Suzanne went on. "I don't know how to stop it."

She saw the moment Lance realized she wasn't just talking about a dream anymore. An instant later, she felt the swirling chaos of his response. His emotions, both positive and negative, slammed into her, nearly making her lose control of her own. As she struggled to maintain her grip, the redcap reared up and flooded her with malice and hate and murderous intent. Before she could regain control, she felt her shoulder fins unfurl, spying their reflection in the mirror. Black as pitch and crimson red. Crackling with such power as they never had before. For the briefest instant, she reveled in the strength coursing through her. Strength her father would have respected... strength he would have feared. Enough power that none would dare to threaten her ever again or try to subject her to their will.

Enough power for her to realize the lie in that truth.

She could give in to the redcap and be as powerful as this and more, at the cost of all that made her decent and good. At the cost of her love and compassion. For the blood-price of her husband and anyone else caught within her sphere. For the blood-price of her child, who would never survive Suzanne's downfall.

No fucking way in hell!

At one time in her life, she believed she needed to take on the world on her own. That to be strong was to stand alone. Very recently, she learned how wrong that delusion was.

Breathing deep, Suzanne reached for Lance across their inner bond, wordlessly asking for his help, his strength, not because she wasn't strong enough on her own, but because they were stronger together. She showed him with her mind what she planned. Mage energy and empathy intertwined. Suzanne let the positive emotions wash through her: reaching for Lance's joy and love, for her unborn child's trust, for the sheer wonder she herself felt deep inside. She anchored the positivity deep in her core, wrapped it around their child stronger than any armor. The extra power unfurled around her much as her shoulder fins had, the energy nearly overwhelming. She felt Lance entwine with her, a counterbalance as she harnessed the energy, forcing the negativity back, breaking its hold. With her thoughts, she followed the link to the redcap and tugged on it hard.

The creature's shriek rang through her mind as he fought back. He tried to tear through her soul, pummeling her with every doubt, every insecurity she ever felt. Feeding her more that had never even occurred to her. For once and for good, she knew it all for lies. She stood like bedrock against the redcap and let the negativity flow off of her like weak water. When she'd had enough, she reached out her will and gripped the tether linking them and squeezed.

*This is not your bed,* she hissed in her thoughts, *This is not your life, and if you try to claim it, I will burn you to less than cinder and ash,* she continued as she forced the presence of the redcap away, barring it from her innermost being, all but severing the connection between them until nothing but the slightest thread linked her psyche to the parasite. That too would be broken if she'd only herself to suffer the consequences.

The war was not over, but this was a battle won.

# About the Author

AWARD-WINNING AUTHOR, EDITOR, AND PUBLISHER DANIELLE Ackley-McPhail has worked both sides of the publishing industry for longer than she cares to admit. In 2014 she joined forces with husband Mike McPhail and friend Greg Schauer to form her own publishing house, eSpec Books (www.especbooks.com).

Her published works include six novels, *Yesterday's Dreams, Tomorrow's Memories, Today's Promise, The Halfling's Court, The Redcaps' Queen*, and *Baba Ali and the Clockwork Djinn*, written with Day Al-Mohamed. She is also the author of the solo collections *Eternal Wanderings, A Legacy of Stars, Consigned to the Sea, Flash in the Can, Transcendence, Between Darkness and Light*, and the non-fiction writers' guides *The Literary Handyman , More Tips from the Handyman*, and *LH: Build-A-Book Workshop*. She is the senior editor of the *Bad-Ass Faeries* anthology series, *Gaslight & Grimm, Side of Good/Side of Evil, After Punk*, and *Footprints in the Stars*. Her short stories are included in numerous other anthologies and collections.

In addition to her literary acclaim, she crafts and sells original costume horns under the moniker The Hornie Lady Custom Costume Horns, and homemade flavor-infused candied ginger under the brand of Ginger KICK! at literary conventions, on commission, and wholesale.

Danielle lives in New Jersey with husband and fellow writer, Mike McPhail and two extremely spoiled cats.

# OUR SKULK OF SLY FOXES

Anders Håkon Gaut
Anonymous Reader
Aysha Rehm
C.J. Frost
Cato Vandrare
Cheri Kannarr
Christopher J. Burke
Christopher Weuve
Chuck Robinson
Deanna Stanley
eSpec Books
Gary Phillips
Gav
Heather Stephens
Ian Harvey
James Gotaas
Jaq Greenspon
Jen Kappert

Jennifer L. Pierce
Judi Fleming
Judith Waidlich
Kelly Pierce
L.E. Custodio
Lark Cunningham
Lorraine J. Anderson
maileguy
mdtommyd
Mike M.
Peter Engebos
pjk
Scott Schaper
Steph Parker
Stephen Ballentine
The Creative Fund
Tina M Noe Good